NATURAL
INSTINCTS
TALES OF WITCHES AND WARLOCKS

www.zombieworks.us

The characters and events portrayed in this book are considered fictional. But any similarity to real persons, living or dead, is coincidental and not intended by the author.

Zombie Works Publications
21050 Little Beaver Road,
Apple Valley, CA 92308

Copyright 2021 by Edward Ahern . Copyright 2021 by Gabbi Van Amburg . Copyright 2021 by Stephanie J Bardy . Copyright 2021 by Cathy Bryant . Copyright 2021 by Steve Carr . Copyright 2021 by Kevin A. Davis . Copyright 2021 by Dawn DeBraal . Copyright 2021 by James S. Dorr . Copyright 2021 by Peggy Gerber . Copyright 2021 by Dylan James Harper . Copyright 2021 by Stephen Johnson . Copyright 2021 by Donna J. W. Munro . Copyright 2021 by Melissa Small . Copyright 2021 by Victory Witherkeigh .

ISBN: 978-1-7372947-5-7
First Printing October 2021

Zombie Works Publications is a registered trademark of Dark Myth Publications.

Table of Contents

Introduction

Power. The ability to cast magic and bend reality to your will. We've all thought about it. Secretly dreamed of it, hoped that it existed in a boring everyday life. Our mothers fantasized about having the ability to wiggle their nose and all the laundry would be done. Some of us dreamed of being charmed or living in the big old magical but oh so practical house with two crazy aunts. Hollywood made witches and warlocks scary, evil creatures, and as time passed, they made them sensual, alluring and almost innocent. The one thing that never changed was the magic. That ability to change things you didn't like, be it your eye color or the guy you're dating.

The ability to fly, to transform, to mix potions and cast spells has been a popular fascination since before Shakespeare first penned double, double, toil and trouble. We have feared them and wanted to be them. We dress as them for Halloween and turn to them for answers when life isn't so clear. We change the name and call them healers. We use their remedies and still don't understand the true nature of the witch. Are they really magic? Or are they like everyone else, just more in tune with the ebb and flow around them. More connected to their natural instincts. Regardless of what has been believed, or perceived to be believed, no matter how they have been portrayed, witches and warlocks have been everything from a curiosity to a fervent obsessive passion.

Being exposed. It is one of the greatest fears of someone who walks a natural path. I work with energy and can feel the hum and shiver of a forest as it anticipates each season. I can feel the presence of others and have been called witch, unnatural. Yet, to me, to feel that ebb, that flow, to tap into that energy around me, feels natural, instinctual. That makes this particular theme one that is very close to my heart.

As each story came in, as each author was chosen, I felt a sense of magic growing within the pages. Each story carried a tale of one who was either cursed by a witch or warlock, or one who lived under that title. Each story is different from the one before or the one after. Each page holds a tale that captives, fascinates and pulls you in. Just as the lure of magic and power do.

The tales in this book are fiction, but as I read them, I got a sense of each author. How they wrote about the witch or warlock in their tale. Were they persecuted? Were they evil? Was the story an almost personal account of one's life? An experience the author had? Each is so well written that it leaves you wanting more, and again asking that age old question.

Does magic exist? Is it taught? Or is it Natural Instincts.

You decide. You fall into that world and see what you carry with you when you reach the end of this anthology. Step outside, close your eyes and feel the magic of the everyday life around you. As a line from a movie that is a particular favorite of mine says, there is a little witch in all of us.

I promise that Natural Instincts: Tales of Witches and Warlocks will wrap you in the magic of each story, it will pull you into the pages and spit you out at the end entertained and maybe just maybe a bit more curious, a bit more in tune with your own with magic. With your own natural instincts.

Stephanie J. Bardy
October 2021

NATURAL
INSTINCTS
TALES OF WITCHES AND WARLOCKS

The Samhain Show
By: Edward Ahern

BRUNSTELLA SIGHED, WISHING she had gone into dealing drugs. "I can't move the cauldron."

Griselda patted her sister's shoulder. "Of course, you can, dearie. Just use a spell."

"I've only got magick left for one spell. I'm not blowing it on rolling a rusty iron pot out into the woods."

"Then hire a troll."

"With what? Nobody pays us for spells anymore, they've all got miracle cures from pharmacies."

Griselda's voice hardened. "It's the Samhain sacrifice, sweetie, we swore to observe it."

Brunstella grabbed her cane and stood up, joints creaking. "If we cut the baby into quarters, we could just use a stew pot and freeze the leftovers for next year."

"You know better. It has to be a whole, live baby girl, unbaptized. Unbaptized is easy to find these days."

"Yeah, but not so easy to boil. The last one puked in the pot and it took me three hours to clean it out."

Griselda leaned forward to whisper in her sister's ear. "Do be cautious, younger sister. You know who is listening."

Brunstella's laugh was harsh. "When's the last time we saw her? Eighty years? I think she's wagging her infernal booty elsewhere. We're obsolete."

Griselda slapped her, mottling the wrinkled skin of Brunstella's cheek. "Never doubt the Mistress! Just do as she ordered us."

Brunstella muttered but stiffly lowered herself back down to think. If magick was out, she'd have to rely on cunning. I could have done better for myself, she thought, a shill or a prostitute, but look where I am.

Then an idea struck her, and she got up with a groan and hobbled down a dirt track that led away from their cottage, then forked left onto a gravel road for another half mile, eventually reaching a cabin. She walked up to the door and yelled inside.

"Tom, you sober enough to talk?"

"Get away from me, you miserable hag."

"Don't be like that. I need you and your tow truck."

"The last thing I did for you gave me shingles. Go away."

"No, seriously. I can give you erotic visions like a sultan never had."

Tom snorted. "Get out of the dark ages. I've already got four bookmarked porn sites, all free."

Brunstella wouldn't be put off. "Okay, how'd you like to get wasted on the nectar of the gods?"

"Like you knew how to get it." But his tone had

changed, and Brunstella knew she had him interested.

"It's an old family recipe. All you have to do is move something and I'll give you enough divine booze to stay blasted for a week."

The door cracked open, and a blotchy, bleary-eyed face appeared. "Move what?"

"Just a big old stew pot. I need it to go into the woods, then a few weeks later to be lugged out.

"How big?"

Brunstella's first instinct was to lie, but she knew he'd find out anyway. "Maybe four hundred pounds."

"That's not a pot, that's a hot tub. Make it enough booze for two weeks."

Brunstella didn't hesitate. "Done! It'll be ready for you day after tomorrow when you come to move the cauldron."

She hobbled back down the gravel road but stopped just before the turnoff onto the dirt track and went up to a one wide trailer that hadn't moved or been improved for a quarter century. The makeshift wood steps up to the door were almost rotted through, and she stepped carefully, then knocked. "Craig! It's Brunstella. I got a deal for you."

"Get away from my door or I'll be the one cursing you."

"Now, now Craig, I think I can take that contaminated moonshine off your hands. Maybe even pay you a little."

Craig, who considered himself an unappreciated cinematographic genius, cracked open the door and peeped at her. "It's got turpentine spilled into it, you old biddy, nobody could abide the taste."

Brunstella smiled. "Yes, well by the time I've added in herbs and hallucinogens it'll taste like nectar. You still got it?"

"Yeah." Craig opened the door all the way and let her in. "How would you move it?"

"I'll come by later on with a wheelbarrow." She looked around the room. Everything was gray, hidden under a half-decade of dust. Everything except a small desk with a lap top computer and sheets of paper. "Working on something?"

Craig's shoulders sagged. "I got an in at a studio, producer named Harry Beerstein owes me a favor, but I need a concept for a TV show, and my mind is farting bad scenarios."

That's when Brunstella had her second great idea of the day. She stood still for several seconds, thinking it through.

"You've been living so bad you might as well have been cursed, Craig, but I've got your cure."

"I doubt you've even got money for the booze."

"Hear me out. Reality shows are what everybody's watching right? We give 'em the ultimate- intrigue, hatred, nudity, promiscuous sex, violence, even human sacrifice."

"Hah?"

"The Samhain ritual, stupid. We do a bunch of episodes leading up to the sacrifice, shoot it all on your hand-held camera, hire our neighbors in for dirt wages- hell, some of them would do it for free- it's got everything. You just need a watcha-callit- trunk line.

"Log line. Jesus, Brunstella, it just might work."

"Don't bring him into it. Of course, it will. How's this for a log line? 'Hidden witches corrupt their town for devil worship.'

Craig had started pacing back and forth, stirring up dust. "Close. But you and Griselda are toad ugly. Nobody would

4

watch you with or without clothes."

"Don't worry about that. We'd use some of our local sinners for the sex scenes and nude dancing. For the climax episode we'd rent an unwanted infant…"

Craig warmed to the idea. "Then shoot the parents getting remorse and showing up at the ceremony and getting beaten and cursed. All staged of course, but what reality show isn't? Yeah, I like it."

They talked excitedly for another hour, Craig tapping possibilities into his laptop. He was so worked up about the project he gave Brunstella the contaminated hooch for a hair restorative ointment.

Darkness was creeping in as Brunstella limped down the dirt track to their cottage. She knew she couldn't tell Griselda, not yet anyway. Griselda was the conservative witchy equivalent of Opus Dei. As she entered the cottage, lit only by firelight and candles, Griselda was skinning a cat.

"Ritual?" Brunstella asked.

"Supper," Griselda replied. "What about the cauldron?"

"Taken care of. You and I are going to Craig's tomorrow with the wheelbarrow and picking up two cases of poisoned booze. I doctor the booze and give it to drunken Tom, who'll use his tow truck to carry the cauldron into the woods."

"We don't have money for that, and you've got no powers right now. How'd you do it?"

"Grace and kindness. Don't' worry, it's done."

"Tom's apt to die or go crazy."

"Yup."

"Okay. Supper'll be ready in a half hour."

Griselda and Brunstella picked up and doctored the moonshine the next morning and delivered it to Tom. Craig showed up at their cottage two days later. He was afraid to go up to the cottage door and called out from down the path. "Brunstella!"

She heard his third yell and came out, putting a finger to her lips, then walking with him into a shaded grove. "What news?"

"He liked the idea. Said it was fresh, edgy. But he doesn't know you. Or trust you. He needs some footage to show what we can do."

Brunstella nodded. She appreciated doubt and suspicion. "Your camera and mic working?"

"Sure. What are you thinking of?"

"Tom's hauling a cauldron for me. You and I go with him into the woods, along with that skank girlfriend of his. You're filming all the way through. I do some smoke and haze mumbo jumbo over a bottle of the booze and give it to them. They'll start drinking, it's what they do. Then you shoot whatever else they do, truck bed, hood, front seat, whatever. There'll be enough Spanish fly in the bottle to kill the bull it was meant for."

"What if they die on the hood?"

"Doubt it, those pickles left cucumber behind a long time ago. But just keep shooting. They're apt to drool, so get close enough to show the spit bubbles. Then I step in, yell some nonsense, and administer an antidote."

"Antidote?"

"Just an emetic, ilex vomitoria. But their spew should be good footage."

"I can't do that to Tom."

6

"Tom does it to himself all the time. Besides, he probably won't remember. And you've got the almost porn that could get us the show."

"That's pretty vile."

"I know. Fun, isn't it?"

And so, it was scripted, and so it was done. And edited. Tom displayed remarkable staying power and inventiveness. Craig was just clever enough to put the footage on a website with one-time, protected access, so his close friend couldn't shop the idea around and double cross him. Harry Beerstein called back two days later.

"Brilliant work, Craig, brilliant. But I need a copy so I can show it to the right people."

"That's great, Harry. But first things first. I need you to option the concept for say thirty grand. I've drafted and registered a little something I'll send you. As soon as we're in binding agreement I'll be glad to send you a tape for circulation."

Harry got peeved, yelling that Craig was grievously lacking in talent and that his ancestry was subhuman. But once Harry saw that his bullying was having no effect he quieted down and agreed.

Craig went into town and bought a burner cell phone, then turned around and drove down the dirt track to Brunstella's cottage.

She saw him coming and hobbled out. "Do I need to curse him with boils?"

"Nah, he's sending the thirty thou, enough to get started. Look, here's a cell phone. I'll show you how to use it."

"I can't. We hold to the old ways."

"And I'm not going to shag my ass down here every day

just to talk with you. Considering how it's used I'm pretty sure this is an invention of the devil."

Brunstella had thought Craig through. So long as he was straining for ego gratification and money, he'd be an adequately bad boy. But once he'd arrived as a movie maker Brunstella was going to have to short leash and muzzle him with a nice disfigurement curse. "So, what's next, Craig?"

"Beerstein will put together a promo piece using some of our edgier footage and shop it around to investors. He hopes to get the up-front money commitments a few weeks after that. You're going to have to tell Griselda then."

Brunstella spat yellow. "I know." As they kept talking, they walked in a circle out to Craig's one wide and back. As they re-approached the witches' cottage, Brunstella's insides felt like they'd curdled into corpse rot. "Somethings wrong," she told Craig. "Get out of here. Now. I'll call you on that flapdoodle."

She hobbled gingerly up to the cottage door and entered. Griselda faced her, both arms akimbo, broken into odd angles. Witches can't cry, but Griselda's sweaty skin and rheumy eyes told of great pain. "What did you do, you clapped out whore?" Griselda demanded.

Brunstella hobbled one step toward her sister, then stopped. Something was sitting in the chair next to the fireplace.

"Yes, Brunstella, what did you do?"

The greasy voice poured over Brunstella like burning oil. Which was okay, really, because she did the same thing recreationally. "Mistress."

"I leave you two to quietly corrupt into dust and you cause trouble with my new projects."

"Mistress?"

"That bulbous letch Beerstein is shopping around a Samhain concept for a reality show. That's something just between us girls. I've devoted too much time corrupting this nation to have it interfered with by Amateur Hour."

The Mistress' words were soft pitched and calm and coated in venom. Griselda had started to whimper. Brunstella's mind churned desperately, and she pulled together fragments of what Craig had told her. "Mistress, you have been so busy damning the mainstreams that you haven't had time for the tributaries."

The hand on the arm of the chair turned into a claw, mostly blotchy blue. "Explain yourself."

"Just market segmentation. Griselda and I are traditionalists, we understand the part of the viewing audience that still watches televangelists."

"So?" The word dripped acid.

"The Samhain reality show will apparently condemn wanton, infernal behavior, but will show it in such an attractive way that the religious will be curious. If they're curious they're halfway to you, a large group you're not reaching with your current programming."

The thing in the chair smiled. It wasn't pleasant.

"Brunstella, you wart plantation, you're onto something. Needs work of course, some demonic script writers, ads in church bulletins, that sort of thing. But yes, maybe. You're coming to Hollywood. But I can't have anyone as ugly as you working for me or having a lead role. Hold on."

Brunstella dropped to the floor writhing in pain. Everything, even her teeth hurt like heaven. When she stood up again, she was thirty something with fully working, reasonably attractive parts. "Thank you, Mistress."

The thing in the chair glanced at Griselda. "A theatrical career requires personal sacrifices Brunstella. I'll need to shut down your little operation here. Are you willing to dump Craig and abandon Griselda?"

Brunstella considered the alternative. "No problem."

Edward Ahern

Ed Ahern resumed writing after forty odd years in foreign intelligence and international sales. He's had over three hundred stories and poems published so far, and six books. Ed works the other side of writing at Bewildering Stories, where he sits on the review board and manages a posse of nine review editors.

https://www.twitter.com/bottomstripper

https://www.facebook.com/EdAhern73/?ref=bookmarks

https://www.instagram.com/edwardahern1860/

Hatless Witch
By: Gabbi Van Amburg & Dylan James Harper

THE KNIFE PLUNGED into Mr. Prescott's arm; blood began to trickle onto the floor. The knife moved slowly up from his wrist until it reached the vein inside the elbow. The trickle was now a flow, and Mr. Prescott, already a pale man, looked even more translucent than usual.

"I have only moments before my volunteer will perish," Vanessa announced to the class in the voice of an experienced performer.

"Not to fear; should I fail Madam Shipton is standing by, but I am confident I will not need to call on the remarkable skill of our principal."

Vanessa opened her satchel and pulled out a white wax candle, a brass holder, and a glass jar. With a wave of her hand, she summoned the knife back, and made a runic insignia of her own design into the candle with her right hand, before lighting the wick with a flare of her left.

Quickly, pulled out a small clay pot filled with soil, and casually made it hover over the flame before opening the glass jar, effortlessly tossing tiny seeds onto the soil.

After tossing the glass jar and the knife back into her bag, Vanessa took a deep breath and brought both her hands back, like a trebuchet being loaded to fire. With a flourish, she brought both arms forward, causing the candle flame to erupt and several green vines to shoot out of the pot.

As the vines shot upwards, Vanessa made a wrapping motion with her hands and the vines mimicked her, wrapping around each other as they climbed. At the top, they fused, forming a vibrant blood red flower that opened up with two large petals, forming what looked like the mouth of a hungry predator.

"Mr. Prescott, please insert your arm into the flower," Vanessa commanded.

Mr. Prescott, who had been slouching in a small chair, tried to stand, but quickly plopped back down. A short, squat woman with gray hair wearing a black cape to match her pointed hat and holding a raven-head cane began to stand up, but Vanessa quickly waved a hand to have her sit back down before dashing around the table to help Mr. Prescott.

Vanessa carried him over and delicately placed his arm inside the flower, which clamped down. Everyone in the audience, save for the squat woman, gasped. A golden glow emanated from inside the flower, which flashed rapidly before Vanessa waved her hands, spreading them apart in the air, causing the flower to open. Mr. Prescott took his cue and held up his now fully healed arm.

The crowd erupted in applause, and Vanessa bowed. Mr. Prescott, who had joined in the clapping, stopped to grab her hand, and hold it up in triumph. She nodded at him and mouthed her thanks before the crowd fell silent.

14

Vanessa turned to see the squat woman had stood and made her way to the front. Her high-pitched voice cut through the room easier than Vanessa's knife into Mr. Prescott's arm.

"The soil was preprepared, when it should have been summoned, unless you plan on carrying around soil with you at all times," she remarked.

Vanessa started to reply, but Mr. Prescott put a hand on her shoulder, and she fell silent.

"And if my dear friend Methais hadn't summoned the energy to make his way to the flower, I fear he would be decomposing as we speak," she added.

The crowd remained silent, waiting feverishly for a summation.

"That said, I think we all just witnessed a witch earn her hat," the woman concluded.

The crowd again began to cheer, and Vanessa, now blushing redder than the flower, put her hands to her mouth in jubilation.

"Thank you Principal Shipton!" she finally said,

Tabby ran through the crowd to her friend.

"You were amazing!" she cried, pulling Nessa in close.

"Thank you so much, I can't believe it," Nessa replied, pulling back to smile at her friend.

"Yeah, nice job babe," a casual voice yawned. A tall blonde boy, looking like a bean pole, had walked up as well.

"Thank you, Rory," Nessa added, reaching over Tabby's shoulder to clasp his hand.

"I'm very proud of you," Mr. Prescott mentioned, as he began to walk off.

"Thank you so much, you were the best mentor," Vanessa said quickly.

"You made it easy. Don't forget, just because you finished your final presentation, I still expect you in class on Monday." He strolled off, arm in arm with the principal.

After Nessa's bag was packed up, she, Rory, and Tabby walked off together out of the classroom and into the fresh night air.

"I gotta tell my grandpa before we leave campus," Nessa said, and waved her hands causing a red spark to shoot up into the sky and off in the direction of her grandfather's house.

"One down, one to go," Rory said, eyeing Tabby.

"Ugh, don't remind me," Tabby whined.

"Any luck with your final?" Nessa asked, hopefully.

"No, the little bastard won't show up; it's so hard being a Shackler," Tabby complained.

"All the fields have their challenges," Rory replied.

"Oh please, your final Astrology presentation was just telling Principal Shipton that Mercury's convergence meant she would get heartburn if she ate the rest of her leftover burrito," Tabby argued.

"Good enough to get my hat," Rory chuckled.

"Apothecary does seem really complicated," Tabby added quickly, not wanting to take away from Nessa's moment.

"It can be, but Mr. Prescott was so helpful; I wish you had an actual Shackler to mentor you," Nessa said comfortingly.

"Yeah, it sucks that it's so rare," Tabby confirmed.

16

"Alright, we're gonna walk around some more and you're gonna head home to practice," Rory announced.

"Is that an astrological prediction or a hint that you two wanna make out?" Tabby laughed, elbowing Rory in the ribs.

"Yes," Rory replied.

Tabby waved goodbye and split off, the anxiety increasing as she put more distance between her and her friends. When she got home, she sat down at her large wooden desk and pulled out her boline. The desk was covered in the etchings of failed attempts to summon a demon, and without a hat she wasn't able to use magic off school grounds to wipe the markings away and start fresh.

"Ugh," she groaned, putting her head down on her desk.

She put away the boline and pulled out a notebook, starting her essay on the five most powerful sea witches in history; another thing that would have been easier if she could use magic. Eventually, she fell asleep at her desk, halfway through another essay on the founding of their town of Dogsmouth.

Paralyzed by a fear of failing, Tabby spent the weekend not practicing, instead doing menial tasks as her joy for Nessa soured with envy.

The dreadful thought of Nessa galivanting around town, with a brand-new witch's hat, while Tabby sat in the remedial licensing summer lessons kept intruding on her as she approached campus.

"Tabby baby!" Rory called out from around the corner.

"Hey Rory," Tabby called back, trying to hide her dread.

"Hey, this is gonna sound weird, but I was stargazing after Nessa and I - uh - finished," he said awkwardly.

"Is that weird?" Tabby asked.

"No, but like, okay, If you find something on the ground, don't like, ingest it. Don't drink anything that's not yours either. In fact, maybe like, don't do anything," he cautioned.

Rory's vague warnings were commonplace, so Tabby smiled but paid little heed.

"Hey, what's up?" Nessa said, sneaking up from behind both of them.

"How you feeling as a soon-to-be-hatted?" Rory asked.

Tabby sped up a bit.

"Honestly, amazing. It's nice to have this load off," Nessa replied.

"Hey, I'm gonna run ahead and get some practice in before class," Tabby said quickly, already practically jogging to get ahead of them.

"Wait, Tabbs," Nessa tried to call, but Tabby was too far ahead and kept going.

She pretended like she was going to the lone Shackler practice room, but as soon as she was out of sight she ducked into the nearest bathroom, close to tears.

"Hey, watch it!" came a raspy voice, just inside the bathroom door.

"Oh sorry," Tabby said, dodging a willowy girl in a loose linen kaftan that made her nearly shapeless.

"Nah, it's cool," said the girl, blowing a smoke ring out of her mouth. It looked extremely cool.

"I think we have sixth period together," the girl added casually.

"Oh yeah, probably, I usually can't pay attention by sixth, I'm so exhausted," Tabby replied.

"I'm Alis," the girl offered.

"Tabby."

"Oh yeah, the Shackler!" Alis replied enthusiastically.

"Well, not much of one," Tabby said, now wiping her eyes in the mirror.

There was an awkward pause as Alis took another drag off a long white pipe.

"It's gotta be hard to be the only one on campus." Alis tried to be comforting, which Tabby appreciated.

"Yeah, and no mentor."

"That's not even fair," Alis commiserated.

"Right! How am I supposed to practice summoning this fucking demon AND do all my homework without magic?" Tabby whined.

There was another pause as Alis blew another smoke circle.

"How do you feel about cutting?" she asked casually, as if she had asked about the weather.

"What?"

"Like, class?"

"Oh, uh, I guess I've never done it?"

Alis tossed her pipe into her satchel, then reached out and grabbed Tabby's hand.

"Let's go, I've got an idea." Alis sounded confident.

Tabby feigned reluctance but knew she would gladly go anywhere this girl was going to take her, and after a few head shakes quickly followed. As soon as they left the bathroom however, they bumped into Mr. Prescott.

"Good morning!" he said, a wide smile across his face.

"Tabby, I'm glad I caught you. I wanted to talk to you. Vanessa mentioned that you were having trouble summoning your demon. I'm not a Shackler of course, but if you ever need extra help— "

Alis cut him off, which scandalized Tabby. "Hey, thanks Matt, but we're late for class," she said, pulling Tabby along.

"Oh, well, you know where my office is," Mr. Prescott responded, looking a little concerned.

The pair dodged across the thoroughfare and through some bushes. Once on the other side of the hedge, Alis pulled her pipe back out of her satchel and started smoking again.

"Where are we going?" Tabby badly wanted to impress this girl but was also very afraid of breaking the rules.

"Have you heard of Athane?" Alis asked.

"Yeah, of course, we have a few Athane specialists here, right?" Tabby replied.

"None like who I'm taking you too," Alis smiled.

They walked in silence for a while. Tabby felt uneasy, but she sensed Alis didn't mind too much. After a while they got to talking about school, about their teachers, about magic. Alis was a Kemuri specialist, which, while not as rare as Shacklers, was still not common in Dogsmouth.

"A lot of people don't get what it's like to have only a few people on campus to talk with," Alis said.

"Yeah, I love Nessa, but she's just so perfect and good at Apothecary, and Mr. Prescott seems like such a good teacher to help her. I have no one," Tabby complained.

"Well, I can't help that you're the only Shackler in town,

but I might be able to help give you more time to focus," Alis smiled, gesturing ahead at a grassy knoll.

"Uh?" Tabby started, but before she could ask what was going on, a small round door appeared in the side of the knoll.

It led to an Athane Parlor. Large metallic chairs were aligned like a barbershop, filled with people getting markings on their skin that would enhance their magic in some way.

"Alis!" came a voice from the back.

"Hey, what's up Damek?" Alis called back.

A thin man covered with markings walked over to them, brandishing a short blade with a pearl handle.

"I need you to do a solid for my new friend," Alis said, gesturing at Tabby.

"Oh yeah, what's that?" Damek said, ushering them back to his seat.

"She doesn't have her hat yet, but she needs a little magic outside of school just to get some homework and chores done."

"Just homework and chores?" Damek asked, raising an eyebrow.

"She's not like me," Alis winked at Tabby.

"Alright, sit down little lady," Damek replied.

Tabby sat down nervously.

"So, the way this works is it'll break the spell that stops hatless witches from using magic outside of school, but your body is basically casting two spells for every one. It takes a toll, especially if you aren't used to doing magic regularly, so you gotta take it easy," Damek explained.

Tabby felt like she was being rushed into this a bit, but the allure of being able to use magic outside of school was tempting. Before she could really decide, Damek grabbed her hand and placed it on the arm of the chair.

"You're gonna wanna get some long sleeved shirts." He made a cut a few inches above her wrist.

No blood left her body as the blade moved, making a runic symbol that must have been of Damek's own design; Tabby had never seen it before. The pain was intense, and as soon as she got used to it, he would move to a new location and continue. She let out a sigh of relief as he finally stopped, only to have him start on the other arm. After several agonizing minutes, he finally put his knife down on the silver tray floating next to him.

"Alright, done," he said.

"How do you feel?" Alis asked.

Tabby was looking wide eyed at the two matching large markings on either arm.

"Uh, fine, I guess. It really hurt."

"That wasn't the blade that hurt," Damek said, drawing the blade over his own arm without flinching. "It was your body reacting to new magic."

"Alright, let's get you home so you can rest and then be super productive," Alis said.

"Remember, don't push yourself too hard or shit will get super bad," Damek warned.

Tabby nodded as she stood up with Alis' help. She shuffled out of the door and staggered home. She woke up several hours later, not remembering getting into her bed. She checked her arms and saw they were still marked up. The anxiety of the week was now replaced with eagerness, as she stood up quickly, ready to test out some at home magic.

She decided to start small, and with a sweeping motion, magically wiped her wooden table clean of markings. She jumped, squealing in excitement. She started to grab her notebook but stopped herself and magically called her notebook to her. By waving her finger, her notebook began to fill up with writing. She pulled out another notebook, and began moving like a chorus conductor, writing two essays simultaneously.

After both were complete, she decided to practice summoning a demon, but by the time she brought her boline to her hand, she was a little woozy, and felt pain in her arms. She looked down and was shocked to see that the markings had grown, now past her elbow and nearing her shoulder.

She decided to ignore this for now and etched out some markings on her desk to try summoning a demon. After her first marking she waited patiently, but nothing happened. With the same sweeping motion, she erased the desk and tried again, and again, to no avail. On the fifth try when she went to move her arm, an extremely sharp pain shot through her. Her vision blurred and suddenly she could barely keep her head up.

The markings now covered her entire body, and it felt like they were trying to pull her skin off. The pain was immense. She tried desperately to stay awake, unsure what would happen if she passed out. She forced herself over to the window, pushing through the pain of one last bit of magic, waving her hands to send a message in the form of red sparks off into the night. It was the last thing she saw before her head hit the windowsill as she passed out.

When she blinked her eyes open, she immediately looked down at her arms, which were now free of the markings. She thought this must have been a dream, until her eyes focused on the figures in the room. Principal Shipton was sitting next to her bed, Mr. Prescott behind her. Nessa was on her other side, grasping her hand.

"The rule against magic outside of school isn't because we like making your schoolwork less convenient," came Principal Shipton's high-pitched voice.

"It's for your own protection," Mr. Prescott finished.

Tabby sat up, took several deep breaths, and started to cry.

"I'm sorry, I'm an awful witch. I can't summon my demon, I can't even cheat without being a burden to everyone," she sobbed, burying her face in her hands.

"No, Tabbs," Nessa started, but Principal Shipton held up a hand, silencing her.

"This is my mistake, not yours," Principal Shipton said.

Tabby looked up.

"I should have realized the stress that led you down this path. When you feel up to it, come back to class and come to my office. You and I will work together until we can coax that demon out for your final presentation," Principal Shipton continued.

Tabby gave a very weak smile in reply.

"Vanessa, you stay with her for tonight. Mr. Prescott will come check on her tomorrow," she concluded, standing to leave.

She shuffled towards the door, leaning on her cane, Mr. Prescott behind her; she turned back around briefly.

"You will find your way to your hat, it will just take patience and a willingness to ask for help," Principal Shipton.

Tabby smiled again, widely this time.

Gabbi Van Amburg

Gabbi Van Amburg is a writer from Sonoma County, California. Her hobbies include medieval embroidery, cookie baking, and celebrating Halloween in August. Her favorite flowers are lilacs.

Dylan James Harper

Dylan James Harper is a teacher and writer from Sonoma County, California. When he's not grading papers or evacuating from fires, he's spending time with his wife and their two wonderful pets. His favorite flowers are sunflowers.

Word Witch
By: Stephanie J. Bardy

SHE SAT AT her table and stared out the big bay windows of her apartment. The computer was set up in front of her, music playing softly, and that cursor blinking at her from the blank page. Words were not coming. She had started and stopped about a hundred times so far. Each time, deleting the words. She was a published author, many times over. This was not new for her, but today, the words would not come.

She watched a group of children run by and down into the little park across the street. She loved where she lived. No one knew her. No one had heard of her or knew her story. No one knew her name. Not her real one. They knew the name she gave them. The one assigned at this birth. They knew her nickname, the one given to her by a past lover. But no one knew her real name. No one saw her real face. She liked that.

She had chosen this place, this time, for that very reason. She was tired of running. She had been moving for well over 300 years. When they got to close, she ended that life cycle and started over in another time, another place. This incarnation hadn't been easy. Her time up to this point had been hard and there were a few times she had almost let them catch her, almost given up. There had been a few times she had almost made the decision to start over.

She hadn't. She played it out. Loved, lost, loved again. Made choices, some good, some bad, but for the first time in forever, she had made choices without the thought of the next life in mind. Now she stared at the children and longed for that freedom, that innocence. She hadn't had that in a very long time. Each life she came back with her knowledge, her awareness. She created the spell to be that way. She refused to lose it all. She had tried to share that knowledge a few times, with disastrous consequences. Now she kept it to herself.

Sort of.

She used to weave her magic into poetry. Spinning words into an image in the readers mind, invoking emotion, that she could draw on. They were easy enough to create. Certain words hold power, when woven with others, they create the needed magic.

Word Witch they had called her. She had laughed. If they only knew.

Then she had gotten an itch. In her soul. It started as a small one, just an idea, a thought, a what if. It grew until she had sat down one day, her children playing, and wrote the first chapter of a book. The power she felt coming from those words shook her. She had long forgotten that she possessed that kind of energy, that kind of magic.

Then she met him. Another like her, a Word Witch. She was afraid at first, as they were rare. As far as she had known, all but a handful had survived the flames. They wove those words together. His suggestions, her magic. For a while it was everything, she thought she wanted. Until it wasn't. He was not like her. The darkness that all Word Witches carried was the part he embraced. The part he thrived in. The natural rule, the instinct is to always keep balance. He tipped his scales to far. She fled. A few years later, they found him and took him back. He no longer belonged to part of this world. She was devastated, but a small part of her was relieved. His magic was dangerous. Not for her, not anymore, but she feared for one not as strong.

She put the book away for a very long time. Played with her poetry and drew substance from that. It became almost like breathing for her, creating a poem. Every few years she would revisit the book. The nine chapters. What a powerful number itself, she could feel the pull every time she opened the file. She had shared it with a few friends and family. Her mother was supportive and encouraged her to write more. She knew she had brought a special soul into this life, one that had a purpose, and she knew it came through words.

She had married, had kids, did all the normal things a regular person did. She tried her hardest to live as normal as she could. She had found others who shared her path, but they were new, fresh, and often mistaken on the purpose and use of magic. It was never about wielding power, it was never about creating power or bending energy to your will, it was about becoming part of the ebb and flow that moved around you. When needed, you could use that energy, but you never possessed it. Her energy would mix with the power around her, and she could do amazing things. But she had to keep that hidden. Those in her life didn't understand that part of her. Didn't understand who or what she was. They didn't have the knowledge she had, the centuries of experience. There was no way they could ever know.

So, she became something she was not. Or at least a lesser version of who she was. She worked basic kitchen magic and allowed those around her to call her Hedge witch. She dabbled in salves and tinctures, but not enough to draw suspicion, and she put her words away. Those chapters sat, untouched for a long time. They were a reminder to her that she had walked away from a life she had lived fully, but shortly. She moved in circles, as was her way, weaving the tapestry of a life mundane. Until one thread, one little thread, pulled.

As with all tapestries, if a thread is pulled, the whole unravels. Her well-choreographed, well organized, impenetrable veneer, cracked.

She got up from the table and made herself another coffee. These memories did nothing to serve her now. It was the life she lived now that she needed to protect. To make matter. To make her difference and leave her mark. She wasn't exactly sure when that shift had come. It may have been when the life she was leading became one of friendly camaraderie. It could have been the encouragement of a random stranger, but she began to release short stories to the world. Sending their magic out, feeling the ripples as people read them and reacted. She brought the Word Witch more and more to the forefront. Those in her life who had never seen this part of her rebelled. Until she broke. She attended an event within the magical community and chose to read her words before the people. The strands of magic that flowed from her lips became visual to her. She could see them wrapping around each spectator, pulling them to her. It had overwhelmed her and filled her at the same time. This, this is what she had longed for.

She brought the book back out and it became a force of

its own. She revisited those 9 chapters, revisited the love, the loss all the threads within that tapestry of time. It consumed her, every day she wrote. Every day she stood beneath the old Grandmother Maple in the back yard and drew energy from her. She funneled that magic, that energy into the words she wrote. The closer the book came to an end, the more she felt herself change. It was more of a stepping back into. She opened that part that she had shut away.

She stared at that blinking cursor and wiped a tear from her cheek. She had sat down to write more on the second book in the trilogy that had originally started as one book. She had sat down with a light feeling in here heart, and now, her chest felt tight, her soul ached. A short story, the idea of a short story had propelled her back to these memories. To that place. But to tell that story, she needed to tell the story of her reawakening.

She closed the laptop and gave up for the day, it was not going to come. Not the words she wanted. She was fighting the words that were needed. She was asked for her story. *Her* story. No one had ever asked for her story, and she wasn't sure if he knew what he had asked for. Not entirely.

She had met him by accident. A friend of a friend. When she had finished the book, she had begun the search for an editor. Someone to help her get those words out into the world and give her that final goodbye she ached for. Her friend had dropped the book into his friend's lap. The words, the magic had found another. At first, she had assumed he was just a person drawn into the magic. She became comfortable with him, talking to him, exchanging ideas, as the words were being prepared to be launched.

Then she had felt his energy. She had offered aid the only way she knew how. From a great distance she had sent her power to heal him. Once her power had touched his, a part, almost a whisper, of her energy, had remained. Almost held onto. And she knew. He was one of the old. A weaver of words, and written magic. He was a Word Witch. This caused her to retreat within herself. To again, hide that part of her away. He had no idea what he was. He had lived his life a man, pursuing a career he had no idea why he was drawn too. He released his words not understanding the magic they wove. How was she to continue to be his friend and not be affected by that magic?

She walked over to her bookcase and pulled that book from its place. As she held it, she felt that familiar hum and tingle. It still carried all the magic it had. Maybe more because with each printing, each reading, it fueled the original power. He had made that happen. He had given that magic life. She had created it, but he had added the final piece. The last ingredient to the magic. He sent it out into the world. The power she gleaned from that was incredible. Her well had been near empty for so many decades and with each sale, each read, each person who contacted her to ask for more, it filled it up. Her soul was healing. Piece by piece, her magic was coming alive. Her power, *all* her power, was waking up.

She sat on the couch holding that book and looked around her small apartment. It had brought her here. To this place. She hugged it to her breast and let the tears fall freely now. She had released those in her life that needed to be set free. They had flown but remained within the circle of her love. For once loved, was always loved, just the direction changed. Now alone, within her own space, she created that sacredness which had been lost, she found her center again. The walls hummed with her magic; the floor vibrated. It was again the sanctuary she had had once so long ago. It had not been so when she first set out. Her magic no longer allowing her to lead that life mundane. It had driven her to the arms of her spirit sister. One of magic and strength, of light and fire. Her sister had been the one to hold up the mirror, to make her see. The magic thought lost, the power, the feminine divine, shone just beyond the tears. Her sister didn't know the true depth of what she was doing, no one knew her true power.

She laid the book on the coffee table in front of her and chuckled. Well, no one but him. When they had met in person, the energy and magic had greeted each other like an old friend. She had been surprised. It was different from the other Word Witch. There was a purity to him, an honesty that had been lacking in the last. His innocence had made her laugh, he had no idea. To this day she wondered if he knew. He had been taken aback when he had felt it. Up to that point, he had questioned the connection the two had shared. He had questioned everything. What he experienced, her power, her magic, pulling at his, erased all doubt that such even existed. He still denied his own magic, but he was willing to accept hers. The small bits that she allowed him to feel. The little pieces she showed to him. She still held back her true face, her true name. That was purely for protection. Not just for her, but for him as well.

The one before had known her true name. Not the extent of her power, for she still kept that dampened so she didn't attract Them. But knowing her true name had damaged him. Or so she had convinced herself. Others had tried to tell her different, but she had seen the good in him, before their energies had been combined. After, he became dark, violent, full of rage and an insatiable thirst for more power. He drained her magic, daily, allowing her to refill when he could get no more. When she had nothing left, she had created a disagreement among the ones they shared a dwelling with. Picked at their magic and had used that to retreat to where she had come from. She had severed the tie

35

that had bound the two, and he became lost to her. He became wild after that, uncontrollable, drawing all the attention to him and They had found him. They took his magic and took his soul home.

She needed a shower. Water always soothed her, and it was the one place she could open her shields completely and let all the magic out. Let it mix with the water and flow away. She gathered what she needed and headed down the small hallway. She shot her laptop an angry glare as she walked by it. Why were the words not coming? Why could she not just pluck a few pages out of the ether and be done for the day? It had never been this hard before. Words were her power, her magic. She wove them like fine silk and today they stuck like burlap. Memories bombarding her from all sides. Her sanctuary suddenly felt like a prison.

She stepped into the hot spray of water, lowered her head so it beat down on her, and with a thought brought her full power to the surface. The light flickered just a bit and an almost audible hum radiated from within the walls of the shower stall. The glass doors shook then became still as her magic mixed with the water. She raised her face, water beating down on it, washing away the tears.

She turned so the water now cascaded down her back and she sighed heavily. She knew she could no longer hide who she was from this man. This Word Witch. He pulled and plucked at that insufferable thread and had unraveled the fine tapestry that she has woven to hide. She knew he could call her by her true name. He already knew it. She knew he could see her true face. No amount of hiding had stopped that. She leaned against the cool tile and let the hot water soothe her. She opened that last gate, and the power immediately reached for his. She felt him stumble. She pulled back just a bit and smiled. Not a moment later she heard her phone ding. That actually made her laugh. She knew what it would say. The same thing it always said when she wrapped herself up in his energy like a security blanket.

You okay?

She took one last deep breath, finished washing up and got out. The words that had eluded her, now danced in her head and before her eyes.

Tell this story. Be that witch again. Create the words and spin the magic.

She pulled her pajama pants on, and an old tank top and sat back down at the computer. She picked up her phone and checked her messages.

You okay? was all he had said.

She replied with a yes, an apology for bombarding him, and told him she was writing. He sent her a dancing gif and she laughed. She would read it for him when it was done. She would tell it all, the whole story. Her life.

And she knew.

At the end of it all, when he said her true name, looked upon her true face, listened to the truest words she had ever written, he would know.

And she would remain.

Because he took a chance on a girl with a book.

Stephanie J. Bardy

Stephanie J. Bardy is an accomplished author, poet and editor. She is Editor in Chief at *The World of Myth Magazine* and has held an editing position with them for over 3 years. She is also Editor in Chief for *Dark Myth Publications* and holds a position on the Board of Directors for *The JayZoMon/DarkMyth Company.*

Her published works include *Eternally Bound, Eternally Bound PCE Exclusive Edition, The Chosen, The World of Myth Anthology Volume 3*, all under *Dark Myth Publications*. She also appears in *Full Moon & Howlin: A Werewolf Anthology* and *Monsterthology 2* published by *Zombie Works*.

She has several short stories to her credit on *The World of Myth Magazine*, and several works of poetry.

Sand Witch
By: Cathy Bryant

"**THIS IS OUR** first day out as a proper family together," Dad said to me wearily. "Please make an effort."

"But she's awful."

"No, she isn't. You haven't given her a chance, Lucy. I'm sorry things didn't work out with your mother, but Judy's a part of our family now -"

- and blah, blah, blah. The Speech again, I thought gloomily, pushing a swimsuit and towel into a bag.

"OK," I said grudgingly.

What The Speech didn't allow for was that Judy was an evil succubus who had stolen my father from both me and my mother. We had become invisible, and he only seemed to notice me now if Judy had a complaint to make about me, which she usually had.

She was packing up sandwiches and drinks when I went downstairs with Dad. She looked up at me and asked, "Swimsuit still fit you?"

Her eyes dropped to my stomach, and I felt enormous. I had indeed put on weight recently, and I hadn't been slender to start with, whereas she was one of those enviable slim-but-curvy women.

"It fits fine, thanks," I replied, trying not to let my anger show.

"It won't soon. My little girl's growing up so fast!" said Dad fondly, ruffling my hair. He still thought I was a little kid, though I was 15 and 5'4, 2 inches taller than Judy. I smiled weakly at him as he went to pack up the car.

"I know some excellent diets, Lucy," said Judy, smiling meanly at me. "You know, I'd be fat if I didn't watch my weight very carefully every day."

I wished that the sandwiches would cram themselves into her mouth and choke her; that the chair she perched on would break into sticks beneath her and beat her when she collapsed on the floor. I wished for powers of telekinesis, for a wild poltergeist to express my anger, for anything to fight her.

I couldn't speak. I was trying not to cry. And I hated my fat ugly self as well as her.

Judy's toddler son Ben came into the kitchen, banging his bucket and spade together and singing a happy wordless song.

"Stop that noise!" barked Judy and grabbed his wrist until his face puckered.

He didn't dare to cry, though, even at his age. I had seen what would happen if he did, though my father hadn't: she would shake him, slap him, and then lock him in the wardrobe for an hour or two. I knew she wanted to do the same to me.

The fact that my father didn't believe me when I told him

about the wardrobe was the most painful thing to happen so far. He asked Judy what had *really* happened, his face full of love and confidence in her and disbelief in me, and she played it bewildered and understanding - said I must have seen Ben playing in the wardrobe and jumped to conclusions. Dad gave me a long talk after that, the first version of The Speech. And I knew that I was alone, and that we were all in danger.

So off we went to the coast, one big happy cliché. It was a sparkling day, and despite everything, my spirits rose. I've always loved the beach, from that sensual tingle of hot sand on the feet to the cool rhythmic rocking of crisp green waves. It was my special place.

We all carried bags, towels, and various bits down to the shore, even Ben, who clasped his little bucket and spade. Once he dropped them, but I picked them up quickly before Judy noticed, and handed them back to him. He almost dared to smile at me.

On the splendid gold-silver stretch of sand we spread out beach towels, propped up the umbrella against the cooler, and gave contented sighs as we began to relax. I wriggled my toes deliciously in the sand and felt a delightfully warm sensation flow up my body.

Judy didn't like salt water, saying it was bad for her skin, and she tried to stop me swimming on the same grounds. Even Dad could see how ridiculous that was, though.

"We can't really expect the children not to go near the sea, when we've come to the beach," he protested feebly.

"Ben isn't swimming or paddling," said Judy, but decided to follow it with a cooing, "But I'm sure you're right, darling," as she saw my father's frown.

I wanted the sand to flick into her eyes and oh, bliss - for once my daydream came true. There must have been a waft of breeze that caught the sand just right, and then Judy was rubbing her eyes, spitting, and snarling.

I turned to hide my smile and walked into the ocean. Soon my father joined me, and we raced and played silly games, and messed about happily. It was brief, but almost perfect - I just wished that Mum could have been there.

She would have been, a year earlier. That was before Judy set her sights on Dad and decided to destroy our family, mainly so that she had more people to bully. Yes, I know, relationships are more complicated than that. But there didn't seem to be any complexity to Judy. She was frighteningly all on one level - selfish, dishonest, and cruel.

Soon Judy called us to lunch, though it was a bit early; she probably just wanted to stop us from enjoying ourselves without her.

"I'm not too hungry yet, thanks," I said as Dad rushed to her side. "I'll play with Ben for a while."

This suited Judy as she then got my Dad all to herself, so we were all happy. Ben was sitting as far away as he was allowed, just in sight but in the lee of some rocks. It felt pleasantly private, even if it wasn't.

He was building sandcastles and chattering merrily to himself. He looked at me a little warily - people were bad news in his world - but carried on playing after I smiled and sat down without comment. Smiles were a new language he was just learning, and I wanted him to be allowed to express something for once.

Like many children of cruel or absent parents (his father was dead, and I wondered how he had died) Ben was developing a fine imagination and learning to live in it when he could. His toddler words were half-English, half-nonsense, but all adventure and excitement.

I watched as he filled his bucket, not really full enough, and patted the contents down with his spade, not really hard enough.

Please let it come out perfect. Please let it be smooth, firm, and lovely, I thought.

Well, sandcastles are unpredictable, and the bucket shape slid out beautifully and stood, flawless. Ben crowed and I grinned.

"Are you going to build a moat, and a drawbridge, and turrets?" I asked.

I had been reading a book called The Hungry Knight and the Castle of Cakes to Ben for days, so he knew all the words. He positively gurgled with delight and began to pile sand and fill his bucket and dig, and I hoped that it would come out as like the drawings of the castle in the book as possible.

And it did. I didn't understand at first. My brain refused to translate what my eyes were seeing. But there it was: the big round keep, the drawbridge, the portcullis - how can a portcullis be made of *sand?*

Ben whooped, laughed, and pointed, and I slowly managed to smile back at him as I realized what I was seeing and what it meant.

I was doing it. The sand was obeying my mental instructions.

I tested it then, trying it to its utmost.

Fill the moat under the drawbridge. We need sand pennants waving from the turrets.

And there was the water, bubbling up in the perfect moat that Ben had apparently dug with a couple of vague spade scoops. And there were the pennants, fluttering in the breeze. Sand pennants. And there was no breeze.

Breeze! I remembered the sand flying into Judy's face earlier, as I had wished it to. Thank you, sand, I thought gleefully, a wave of love and gratitude flowing from me. And the sand glistened and danced a little, as if laughing. Was it sentient? Was it something I was projecting? Did it matter?

Ben was utterly lost in joy now, simply grabbing handfuls of sand and throwing them on to see what wonders they would create: arrow slit windows, perhaps, or crenellated battlements. It was pure magic, just as magic should be, I felt, and I didn't interfere until he began to get tired and gasped as if thirsty.

I gave Ben a hug. "Come on, it's lunchtime," I said. "You can come back and see the castle afterwards."

"Lunk," agreed Ben, and held my hand as we walked back to Dad and Judy.

As we approached, I just had time to hear Judy say, "Boarding school would do wonders for her manners," before her eyes flicked open and she spotted us.

"Any food left?" I asked cheerfully, for once not caring what the witch said or wanted. And with a fine seaside hunger Ben and I ate and drank our fill, Judy looking on disapprovingly.

I thought carefully during lunch, planning exactly what I was going to say and do.

"Daddy," I said with my sweetest smile, "I was wondering if - I mean it might be nice if - if you take Ben for a paddle and then Judy and I can spend some quality time together. What do you think?" And I put on a tremulous smile and did my best to look loving and obedient.

He was delighted.

"Marvelous! That's my girl! Come one, Ben, let's get our

feet nice and wet and then you can show me your castle..."

And off they went, hand in hand, happy.

Judy looked at me suspiciously, but when I said nothing, she went on the offensive.

"Lucy, how would you feel about boarding school?"

"I guess I'm too big to lock in cupboards, so this is the next best thing, right?" I replied.

Her face twisted in fury, but she was far too clever to give herself away verbally. Worried about recording devices, I expect; not that I had ever bothered. I knew I'd never catch her out that easily.

So instead, she grabbed my left index finger and bent it back until I couldn't help but moan. Her point made, she let go, while I held my stricken digit and tried not to cry. Her face had remained expressionless, apart from a certain hardness, throughout the process.

"How exactly did your first husband die?" I hissed, unable not to ask.

And she laughed carelessly and gave me a look that was both knowing and pitying and made my stomach go cold.

I knew what I was doing. I glanced briefly over at Ben and Dad, who were off gazing at the castle, and then I grabbed Judy's beach towel and rolled her off it onto the sand.

Swallow her up. Suck her down quickly. And keep her there, deep, for at least a week.

It must have taken about five seconds, no more. She was just righting herself and getting ready to yell at or torture me when she sank down into the sand, away, with barely time for a perplexed, "What - "

And then nothing. So quick. The sand was as smooth

and peaceful as before, the day as brilliant.

I lay out Judy's towel again and sunbathed on mine, enjoying the warmth and the silence, save for the gentle shushing of waves.

Soon Dad and Ben came back.

"That castle is phenomenal! Who helped you? How did you - " Dad stopped. "Where's Judy?"

"Gone to look for a clean enough loo. You know what she's like," I answered, adding " - careful," rather than the "fussy" I had been thinking. I was being a good girl again. Dad accepted it with an "Ah!" and settled into the cradling sand. I made it especially smooth and comfortable for him, and he looked more relaxed than he had since he broke up with Mum.

I knew that soon enough we'd have to be concerned and search, and report Judy missing, but for the moment things were perfect.

Then Ben whimpered and I felt a twinge of guilt - was he missing his mother? But following his gaze I saw that the tide was coming in and was licking at the castle, slowly melting its elaborate ramparts.

Ben set his face, trying not to cry or make a fuss. I reached for him and hugged him gently, stroking his hair.

"You cry if you want to, Ben. Go ahead," I said softly. "You can cry all you want now."

Cathy Bryant

Cathy Bryant has won 29 writing competitions, and had hundreds of pieces published. Her books are: Contains Strong Language and Scenes of a Sexual Nature, Look at All the Women, Erratics, and How to Win Writing Competitions. Cathy also runs the listings site of free opportunities for impoverished writers, Comps and Calls at www.compsandcalls.com/wp

The Book of Isobel Gowdie
By: Steve Carr

SITTING AT A table in the dining car of an Amtrak train, Jules Lowery tightly held against his chest the oversized *The Book of Isobel Gowdie* that he had covered with black felt. Under the covering, creatures from within the book that wanted out, pushed against the cloth, then retreated back into the book to be replaced moments later by other creatures. He nervously sipped his tea from a cup emblazoned with an Amtrak insignia while staring out the window at the snowy landscape. He was attempting to avoid looking at the young woman seated alone at the table across the aisle. She had been staring at him – or more precisely, at what he was holding – and while he doubted, she might be one of the witches from the Gowdie coven, he wasn't certain. As hard as he tried, he couldn't conceal the movement going on under the cloth. It wasn't the type of thing usually seen by a young woman in a dining car of a train whose last stop was Denver and was now traveling across Colorado on its way to San Francisco. He decided her curiosity was warranted, but it worried him, nevertheless. Trying to steady his jittery hand, he placed the cup on its saucer, rose from his seat and left the dining car, watching over his shoulder to see if he was being followed by the young woman.

He wasn't.

Before he opened the door to his sleeping car the hairs raised on the back of his neck and goosebumps formed on his arms. He placed his hand against the door and quickly pulled it away. Ice covered his palm and fingers. "Lucia!" he stammered, the blood draining from his face. He was convinced that the phrase 'colder than a witch's tit' originated from someone who knew her and had been the object of her wrath.

He backed away from the door, turned, and then ran down the passageway to the last car. He shielded the book inside his jacket, raised the collar around his neck, and buffeted by an icy gust of snow flurries, stepped out onto the observation platform. Embracing the book, he flew from the platform and set down in a mound of snow as gently as a butterfly landing on a cotton ball. He had never learned the mastery of controlling the weather, or how to transport himself from one location to the next, so with his shoulders hunched and his head bowed, began to trod through the wind and snow, hoping that he wouldn't have to walk all the way to California. The beaks, heads, talons, and snouts of the creatures in the book were popping in and out, stirred into a frenzied state either by recently having detected Lucia's presence, or by the increased rapid thumping of his heart. They weren't accustomed to one of the Gowdie coven exhibiting so much fear.

#

After four days of trudging through the snow, at midnight, as a full moon shone through blinding snow, Jules spotted a ski cabin that stood alone, surrounded by fields of snow. Its windows were aglow with candlelight. The creatures in the book had quieted, a few only occasionally poking their proboscises or claws out beneath the felt cloth. He adjusted it against his chest and stomped through the snowdrifts to the door of the cabin. He stopped and listened to the sounds coming from inside the cabin, and hearing only the creaking of a rocking chair, he lightly tapped on the door. He heard the sound of footsteps on a wood floor and then the door slowly squeaked opened. The face of the old man that peered out at him was ashen, lined with wrinkles, and spotted with the signs of old age.

"I've been waiting on you," the old man said, gazing at him through black, beady eyes covered with thick cataracts, the look of a very old witch.

"A Gowdie witch!" Jules exclaimed as he recoiled, prepared to be turned into an earthworm.

The old man cackled loudly, his rotten, broken teeth, showing. "Of course not," he said. "For a warlock, your skills leave a lot to be desired."

"How did you know . . .about me being warlock?" Jules answered, feeling the creatures begin to stir under the felt.

"What is the saying? It takes one to know one. I'm Lucius Inholdt. Do come in." He stepped aside and waved Julius in.

A roaring fire in a large stone fireplace greeted Julius as he entered the cabin. The door closed on its own. Julius looked around. The large room was sparsely furnished; a rocking chair in front of the fireplace, a table with two chairs, and a cot along one wall. A black pot filled with boiling liquid hung a few inches above the fire.

"Do sit down and rest a bit before we have a midnight meal of my infamous soup," Lucius said. He snapped his fingers, and a second rocker appeared a few feet away from the other one.

To Jules, nothing about this felt right. Tentatively, he sat in the rocker and apprehensively watched as Lucius sat down across from him. As a large wooden spoon lifted from its hook embedded in the stone on the outside of the fireplace, smoothly glided the short distance to the pot, and began to swirl the liquid, Jules could barely contain the frenetic activity coming from the book. He looked at Lucius. " Your name is familiar to me, but I don't know why."

"I go by two names. Lucius Inholdt and Lucius Hawthorn, Does that ring a bell?"

"You! You're Lucia's husband. No one ever mentions you when Lucia is around for fear of being turned into a wart strategically placed on the end of someone's nose, but in secret we've all heard of you."

"Was Lucia's husband, but that was a hundred and fifty years ago" he said, his mood and tone darkening. "I guess I'm still technically her husband since a witch and her mate never divorce, but like you, she is the reason I live a life in exile."

"How could that be? Haven't you as much power as she has? " Jules asked, truly shocked.

"Now that you're a warlock too, need I remind you that a warlock receives that title because he is a traitor to the coven, the faith of witchcraft. And as you must have learned, no one has more magic than Lucia, or defies her." Lucius took the spoon from the pot and put it to his mouth. Peering over the spoon at Jules, he said, "Stealing *The Book of Isobel Gowdie* was about the most serious offense against Lucia and her coven imaginable." He slurped in the liquid in the spoon. "Mmmm very tasty. Care to have a taste?"

"No than . . ." Jules began but stopped abruptly. "How did you know I stole the Gowdie book? And now that I think about it, when I first arrived you said you had been waiting on me. How did you know I would be coming here?"

Lucius tossed the spoon aside and rose from his rocking chair. "News travels fast, even among the Gowdie coven outcasts. A certain pretty blonde witch, who saw you in the dining car on the train, arrived on my windowsill as a hawk a few days ago to give me the news that you were heading this direction. She was once Lucia's protege, but they had a falling out over my being expelled from the coven. She had traveled back in time and saw what happened to me first-hand and took pity on me. A very talented witch, that one."

Jules began to sweat, from the heat coming from the fireplace, and what he was certain was coming next.

"If you'd be so kind to turn the book over to me without making a fuss, I'd be so very grateful," Lucius said flashing a malevolent smile.

Inside his jacket, under the felt cover, creatures from inside the book were popping in and out of the book's cover as if the pages inside had been set on fire. Jules stood up and began to back away toward the door. "What interest would you have in my possessing the Gowdie book?"

"If I were to return it to Lucia, my own transgressions would be forgiven, and I'd be accepted back into the Gowdie coven."

With a quick jerk of his head, Jules opened the door, turned into a wolf, and with the book held in his powerful jaws, fled the cabin, with Lucius following right behind, soaring above as a large eagle. Jules knew he had used the only spell he was really proficient at, changing into an

55

animal, but the magic would wear off soon and he'd be back to being Jules, the nebbish warlock who in a hundred years of training had mastered little of the art of witchcraft. What's more, he realized if the young witch on the train knew he was heading in the direction of Lucius' cabin, then so did Lucia; she wasn't riding the train to see the scenery.

As Lucius swooped down preparing to dig his talons into the fur on Julian's back, Jules' four paws landed on a patch of ice, sending him sliding across it and over an embankment, just as an arrow made of ice meant to kill him, missed its target, and instead pierced the eagles' chest.

Returned to his human form, with the book concealed inside his jacket, Jules scampered up the side of the embankment and peered over a mound of snow. There stood Lucia holding a bow made of ice. At her feet lay Lucius' remains – a small pile of dust. Her pale face showed no emotion; it was like a porcelain mask, beautiful but cold.

Jules slid back down the embankment. With no energy left to conjure up more magic to turn back into a wolf, in his human form he ran as fast as his feet could carry him across the snow and into a forest of pine trees.

#

Moonlight shone through the trees, casting shadows across the highway where Jules sat huddled on a guardrail, the book held firmly in his embrace. The creatures had not appeared beneath the felt cover for some time. He knew the spell to make a fire, but he feared Lucia would see it. Even if he had regained the strength to change into another animal or bird, there was the book to think about. Few animals that he had the ability to turn into could easily carry a book as large as *The Book of Isobel Gowdie* only. He

56

knew he wasn't that bright, but not able to think of how to continue on left him exasperated. Then, far off down the highway, the headlights of a semi-truck pierced the darkness. Julian jumped up, ran to the middle of the road, and waved one arm while holding onto the book with the other.

The truck came to a stop just a hundred feet from where Jules was standing. The driver turned on the cab lights. The driver rolled down the window and poked his head out. "Where ya headed?"

"San Francisco," Jules replied.

"That's where I'm goin'" the driver said. "Hop in."

Carefully keeping the book hidden inside his jacket, Jules climbed into the cab and settled back.

"My name's Duncan," the driver said in a thick Scottish brogue, offering his large, meaty hand. He had a thick red beard, a large stomach that hung over his belt, and smelled of tobacco and whiskey.

"Jules," he said, shaking the driver's hand. "You're accent. Are you from Scotland?"

"Born and died in Aulderland, Highland, Scotland."

"Died!" Jules paused for a moment and said, fearfully, "Aulderland, Highland is where Isobel Gowdie was burned at the stake for being a witch," he stuttered.

"And I've been traveling the Earth in one manner or another – horses, carts, carriages, boats, trains, planes, cars, trucks, you name it – ever since," he replied with a menacing cackle.

"Are you saying that you're the ghost of Isobel Gowdie?" Jules asked, astonished. "The world of ghosts and spirits and the world of witchcraft seldom intersect."

"Not in my time," Isobel replied. "But you can't imagine my consternation at finally tracking my book down to being in the hands of a witches' coven in your state of New York just to find it had been stolen – by you!" The truck around them disappeared, and the two stood face-to-face in the road. "I want it back," Isobel roared.

Jules felt his knees weaken. The creatures were biting and clawing at the cloth. For the first time he thought he heard them howling and shrieking. "You're dead, what good would the book do you now?" he asked, his voice trembling.

"I must make sure what has been held captive between its covers all these centuries remains there."

At that moment Lucia appeared in the road only a few yards from where Jules and Isobel stood. She glared at Julian, "You fool, you have no idea what you're dealing with." She then turned her icy gaze on Isobel. "That book now belongs to me," she roared. "I'm taking it back with me."

Jules was knocked aside as Isobel's form changed from that of a truck driver to a biker dressed in leather and wearing a helmet. She was straddling a large Harley. "Over my dead body."

Just as Isobel sped headlong toward Lucia, Jules turned and ran back into the woods, leaving behind him a tumultuous cacophony. The combination of fire and ice licked at his back. There was no mistaking it, the creatures could easily be heard emitting a chorus of animal and bird cries filled with rage.

#

Three days later, in the form of an opossum, Jules left the woods and walked into a cornfield covered in snow and ice. He carried the book on his back, strapped there by dead vines. He quickly chewed through the vines, transformed back to his human form, picked up the book, and marched off toward a farmhouse just beyond the cornfield. It looked safe enough, he thought, but he tried to steel himself for the unexpected. He had his eye on an old car that sat in the driveway beside the house. It looked in good-enough shape to get him the rest of the way to San Francisco. While using a spell to change into an animal was simple enough when used sparingly, only witches at Lucia's level could use a spell to conjure up a car. He did have other small spells up his sleeve that he could cast, in emergencies. He reached the front porch when the door swung open and a man in overalls came out with a rifle pointed at him.

"Who are you and what do you want?" the man asked, brusquely.

Jules opened his hand. In the palm there was a stack of thousand dollar bills. "I need a car and will pay you everything in my hand for yours."

Fifteen minutes later with the car signed over to him, Jules drove away with the book lying in the seat next to him. *That farmer is in for a surprise when the cash vanishes and my signature disappears from the paperwork,* he thought.

#

Driven nonstop and fast, the car finally died in downtown San Francisco, on Market Street, where the radiator cracked, and oil shot up from under the hood and covered the windshield. It was early morning, and the street was shrouded in heavy fog. He grabbed the book and left the car alongside the curb in front of a fire hydrant where it had rolled to during its final motorized gasps. He had memorized the address of where he was taking the book and using a San Francisco guidebook map he quickly walked the three blocks south of Market Street.

The shops name, La Voison Rare Books, was burned into a piece of wood that set in a small display case filled with dust. He rang the door buzzer several times before the door opened.

"Jules Carthill, I presume from your selfie you sent me," the old woman standing in the doorway said, eyeing him up and down. "Did you bring *The Book of Isobel Gowdie?*"

"Yes, to both questions," he replied. "You're Claudine La Voison, the head witch of the La Voison coven?"

She nodded and waved him into the shop, closed the door, and turned on the lights. The rows of shelves and the old books on them were as dusty as the display window.

"Give me the book," she said, holding her hands out.

The creatures had grown calm and quiet. He handed it to her. "Why is this book so important that you would offer me a coven of my own if I took it from Lucia and brought it to you."

She laid it on the top of a dust laden desk. "Inside it are all the other witches Isobel Gowdie imprisoned within its covers before she was put to death, and the coven leaders since then have refused to release. I'm going to free them."

Suddenly panicked, Jules cried out, "Won't they unleash horrors like pestilence, plagues and tribal warfare the world hasn't seen in hundreds of years?" He grasped the edge of the desk as his legs buckled. "They might even kill any other coven leaders who oppose them, including me."

"Probably so," she said as she opened the book.

60

Steve Carr

Steve Carr, from Richmond, Virginia, has had over 560 short stories published internationally in print and online magazines, literary journals, reviews and anthologies since June, 2016. He has had seven collections of his short stories published. His paranormal/horror novel Redbird was released in November, 2019. He has been nominated for a Pushcart Prize twice.

Ruined
By: Kevin A. Davis

I WANTED TO send a flaming ball into the back of Valerie's chatty head, our long journey had tested my tolerance.

She was annoying, like so many entitled mages, but we were at least of the same order. Her ability to talk needlessly and endlessly annoyed me. I rarely enjoy conversations with fellow mages who thought themselves above the banal masses. We thought ourselves enlightened.

"Atahm, are you listening?" she asked.

"Of course," I lied. I was anxious to arrive at our destination and finish this charade. My cloak itched; the heat made me sweat. My hair hung in black ringlets, sticking on my cheeks. These tunnels smelled of damp must, and the air felt stagnant.

I was providing an illuminist's orb for light. It hovered just above and to the right of my head, keeping the light out of my eyes, and throwing my shadow across the stone walls. The pale blue light did nothing to brighten the drab and sometimes moldy stone. The corridor had been carved in a rough tube, like a sewer pipe; the shape giving an illusion of size while only leaving room to walk single file. The bottom of the curve barely measured a step wide, but the overall shape left plenty of room for hands to send bursts of magic from the caster's sides. The walls had been chewed nearly smooth by some conjurer's pet, apparent by the fingernail-sized toothmarks that feathered the stone.

We had been walking for an hour through winding tunnels, public tourist paths, and secret ruins toward our destination. Which was evidently under Ordensburg Vogelsang. Valerie walked ahead flipping her shoulder-length strawberry blonde hair over her shoulders to check my face as she spoke, thus constantly. I wondered if she might give herself whiplash. Her wide fleshy face jostled with the movement, whipping her jowls and thick lips about. Her round, silver-rimmed glasses hung on like an American cowboy astride a rather wide mount.

Her plump fingers, tipped with colorful rainbow nails, touched the side of her mouth.

"The Council is losing. Castigo gains ground, if not by recruiting followers, then by attrition, as our numbers decline," she said. "We are losing."

"It's not that bad," I said, trying to stay attentive to the natter this time.

Her quick glance conveyed her shock. "It is."

Without warning, she turned right down a side corridor. Her pale green cloak swept to one side.

"Joa sacrificed herself during the attack last fall by Castigo's followers. Aemin was cursed in his own bed right before the winter solstice. Then Yailista disappeared just last month. She's dead, surely." Rings glistened in the blue light when she lifted her hands in a sign of distress. "Any of us would sacrifice ourselves to fight this threat, but how many can we afford to lose before Castigo overwhelms the Council?"

"I can't say."

Yailista *had* been a surprise. The Council had remained implacable, certainly.

Another of Valerie's quick turns caused me to stumble in these intolerable sandals. I had to clutch at my gray cloak before I tripped.

"We'll all do our part, to the end." She managed a confident nod as she glanced back. "You're certainly doing yours. Castigo lusts for the Auspice." Her tone became harsh. "Curse Grigori for creating it." She took an extra moment to lock eyes with me. "If Castigo believes you have it, then you might be the next sacrifice."

"I'll keep it safe," I said.

Valerie slowed as we approached a corner in the corridor, but instead of turning we stopped.

Her hands glowed, trailing blue coruscating mist as she dug a long red nail into the stone. She wrote the runes slowly, unlocking a spell likely placed there by a cadre of mages. A proper glyph is a series of runes giving directions, like words forming a sentence, a math equation, or a scientific formula. Add the wrong number and you get the wrong answer.

Despite her focus on an intricate glyph, Valerie turned and smiled. "At least Castigo has brought us back together. No more fragmented orders within orders. No more bickering and infighting. There hasn't been a death outside those that Castigo caused since this whole mess started up."

True.

I preferred to not work with other mages unless they

worked for me. Even then, I would never have suffered this much prattle. She needed to focus.

"Reveal. Unlock Divinity. Pass these two," she wrote.

Her glyph flashed and remained in the air while the rough, indigenous stone faded into mist, leaving a sickly green arch of gaspeite.

She grunted in satisfaction, wiping blue wisps off her hands, and strode through. "Be careful, follow my steps. We've set much here, in case of betrayal."

I followed quickly, careful to match her steps and memorize them for the return.

She swirled her pale red hair as she spoke. "If Castigo captures the Auspice, we believe he has plans to use it beyond our understanding."

Which won't be hard. The Council had little imagination.

"Undoubtedly," I said. The Council, and those who ruled it, had limited, petty minds. They couldn't see beyond their restrictions and traditions.

"The most we've ever been able to get from the Auspice is a few hours of divination into the future." Valerie waved her hand in the air, red nails glinting purple in my orb's light. She turned and scowled, as much as her face would allow. "Grigori supposedly used it for much more, which is why we keep it protected."

"I've heard."

The tunnel turned smoother and wider at the base, but the walls had cracks and moisture trickled down from a crevice.

Wearing a broad, devilish smile, she turned toward me. "Can you imagine our mentor's face if she saw us working together now? She'd not believe it." Valerie raised her eyebrows.

Indeed, Valerie and I had been at odds even then. We'd learned together and from each other, but I had never able to stomach being around her. Nor many of our cadre, for that matter. I'd become solitary as quickly as possible, maintaining my position on the Council by the sheer magnitude of my power. She'd risen, always liked and affable.

"Hmph."

Valerie laughed and swayed down the corridor. "Don't be such a grump, Atahm. I consider it an honor to be part of this. The willingness to sacrifice for a greater cause. You and me. Stopping Castigo."

Her constant optimism grated.

"You can count on me."

"I hope so. But be warned, we've got confirmation that Castigo is one of our own. That's why it's so important we take care of this now." Valerie looked at me, her plump lips pressed together. "None of us are safe. Can you imagine if he had the Auspice? It's only a matter of time before Castigo learns of its location. They are close."

I frowned; I had not heard of their suspicions.

"How do you know?"

"We discussed the concern in open council, which you know, and then we three, myself, Yailista, and Lopine, continued in closed circle inside a ward." Valerie tilted her head with an annoyingly coy smile. "With one aim."

She paused at an intersection where one thin, dark corridor rose on the right.

My ward hummed against my stomach; at least three banes crossed the intersection. My orb scattered light down the halls. No end in sight.

That conversation had become a concern. Of course, I'd listened in on their closed meeting, and knew exactly what they had discussed. Had they prepared this trap for Castigo? If so, I had obliged, though they had no possible way to link me. Still, I had been suspicious when they selected me to protect the Auspice, so I had prepared.

I dropped my right hand into my pocket. I held the poppet and braced it between my thumb and fingers. One wrong move and Valerie would be dead where she stood. It would come to this in the end, but I preferred to have the Auspice in hand before that moment.

She turned, silently urging me to ask about their plan.

I tilted my head toward the plump woman's face. "Yes," I said, prompting her to continue.

Now, the corridor widened into a room, and she carefully chose her steps. I followed. Rough stone floors became massive blue marble paving stones. I only stepped on those she did and memorized each one. The air smelled like a fresh lightning strike, and metal that I could taste on my tongue. We were close. Substantial magic lay ahead.

She continued into the room, where it widened until the blue light of my orb no longer reached the walls.

"We mentioned the location as being in the caverns to the southwest of my workshop."

Yes. I'd searched that rat-infested muck for most of a day. Not even one note of magic had resonated in the vicinity. Except for Yailista, whom I had considered a momentary obstacle, an opportunity to thin their ranks further. A good sign, I had hoped. It had all been a trap to determine that Castigo sat on the council. I had considered that, and they had learned that much, but surely not my identity. There had always been suspicions, openly voiced. Little had been lost.

I waited for her to continue. She motioned toward a pedestal and led the way. "Over here."

My heart began to race in anticipation, and I subdued it with a whisper. Calmly, I followed her. I paced my steps with hers, moved agonizingly slow toward my goal.

The Auspice hung on a carved stone neck. Inauspicious in its appearance, it rang with magic. A flattened gray lump of metal. Featureless, it looked unfinished. Sweet potato vines braided and threaded through the loop at the top to form a necklace. The blue orb barely reflected off the dull metal as if the talisman-soaked light into itself.

She held it out toward my right side, and I took it with my left, leaving my right hand in my pocket. I still could not trust her. What had her little game with Yailista won them, other than knowledge of Castigo's presence on the council? Nothing that I could see.

It didn't matter. The Auspice now sat in my hand.

My own theories on the Auspice derived from faded scraps of Grigori's handwritten notes on worn vellum. The mages who had discovered the talisman only learned the ability to view their own futures, from hours to weeks ahead, depending upon their strength. Grigori, I believed, used it to divine others' futures. His enemies. He would know where they would be, what they would do. A tool I could use.

Tilting forward through sweet potato vines, I slipped it over my head and let it settle under my cloak.

I couldn't resist, I envisaged my future.

Through dead eyes I looked down on fingers scabbed from scraping. The Auspice hung visible on my chest inside a dirty cloak. Bare feet stuck out from under the hem. Water trickled beside me.

My eyes snapped open, and I glared at Valerie.

She wore a sweet smile on her full red lips. Her hands clasped on her stomach. She stood, unassuming and harmless. But oddly, she wasn't talking. Behind those round glasses, she watched me, waiting. Her eyes. Her iris's, normally blue green, had lines of brown flickering in them.

She'd Joined prior to departing with me. Someone, another of the council, rode her vision, saw what she saw.

They *had* suspected me.

The charade was over. They knew. But they were fools if they thought to trade the Auspice, and Valerie's life, for this information. It wouldn't stop me. The Auspice would instead fulfill my every need. I could dismiss them one at a time. I would know where they would be when they would be alone. My followers would eliminate the most resistant. Those remaining would accept the hopelessness of resistance.

I snapped the poppet and Valerie crumpled to the floor. Even in death, she smiled.

Whatever trap they had laid for me wouldn't work. I flared my wards to the full height of my power and magic ignited from the warded stones interspersed in the room.

I raced across the room with unerring memory of her every step.

How had they known? Did it matter? The Auspice had seen me dead.

No, I had a chance. I had pushed it to more than a month away; I still had time to change the future. I had information to alter events; two important pieces: they had identified me, and this entire charade was a trap.

70

I slowed my pace. I considered every line of magic my wards lit up. My orb burned bright as I studied my movements.

How had my trip to the cavern or Yailista's death identified me as Castigo? Yailista had not seen me before or after she died; her body turned to nothing but ashes. She had sat just inside the mouth of the cavern. A proof, at first, to the veracity of the location. She hadn't been warded. *Bait.* Damn these meddling women.

I had been suspicious, of course.

Valerie hadn't been warded, either.

I slowed further at the water that dripped from the ceiling.

Tempted, I resisted taking the time to view my future again.

The scent of mold hung in the air.

How had they trapped me? I had watched Valerie for magic -- never a flicker after the archway.

Other mages couldn't follow us in, not quickly. We'd both placed wards on the outer doors, specifically to keep me or my followers from coming behind. A precaution which I'd been happy to allow. Yet, that had been part of her plan.

Somewhere here lay a trap.

I took each step cautiously, my memory perfect.

How had they known?

I had fallen for the earlier location, a calculated risk. Prior to my arrival, followers had scouted Valerie's workshop and the surrounding area for two weeks. They'd reported her workshop vacant, lightly stocked, and barely used. Not particularly suspicious, until I found nothing at the cavern.

I had met her and Yailista at Valerie's workshop once, months ago. I'd been invited there with the express purpose of planning a minor mission against Castigo. It had failed, of course. Valerie's workshop hadn't been overly impressive at the time.

I arrived at the intersection where the vicious wards crossed the wrong paths and carefully kept close to the corner. Nothing.

Perhaps, just knowing that Valerie had Joined with another had given me the edge to avoid my future. I resisted looking again.

I thought about our meeting at the workshop, months ago. Had there been some clue? If they had learned my identity then, why not kill me in council? They feared those I already had turned.

Something about that meeting gnawed at me.

I stopped.

Valerie had given me the location to her workshop.

A chill flowed down my back. The workshop that would then be used to refer to another location in a secret conversation. If they met with other council members in different locations each of us would have a separate reference for the cavern "southwest of the workshop." I had never asked my followers about their meetings, their locations. I had assumed.

Concerned about a trap as clever, I practically crawled to the entrance until the green arch of gaspeite stood before me.

The glyph hung in the air, a sparkling light blue.

I placed my hand on it, but the ward resisted. Softly at

first, then with increased pressure turning to solid, impenetrable air.

I reread the glyph. "Reveal. Unlock Divinity. *Enter* these two."

Pass had been misspelled.

A slight twist of the rune and the meaning had changed from "pass" to "enter." A rather large difference when writing a glyph. Especially if one wished to exit.

Valerie had known every step of the way.

So, not misspelled. She had been — clever.

In my haste I'd memorized what I had assumed. No one would lock themselves in by only allowing themselves to enter but never exit.

All that talk of sacrifice. I should have destroyed Valerie long ago. All my plans – ruined.

Kevin A. Davis

Kevin A Davis lives in a little house in the woods of north Florida. Surrounded by moss draped live oaks where red-winged hawks pester the neighboring Ents. Books and art cover the walls, and cats dwell upon the surfaces.

He travels to Cons, writing conferences, or helps his wife vend handmade steampunk jewelry. He often wears a kilt and always a hat during such occasions.

Writing in Fantasy (Urban, Epic, Gaslamp), he is on course to self-publish the beginning of an Urban Fantasy novel series in 2021. He writes an occasional short story when an idea burrows into his brain and won't leave on its own. In the meantime, he and his wife have opened a used book store in a sleepy town where they carry the occasional new indie book.

https://www.facebook.com/KevinArthurDavis/

https://kevinarthurdavis.com/

Witch's Code
By: Dawn DeBraal

"**OPEN UP, OLD** woman!" Garth, the tax collector, used his fist on her door, rattling it on its hinges. The old crone opened the door placing a small handful of slugs into the man's leather pouch.

"For King and Crown," she murmured, shutting the door.

The tax collector saw what she had placed in the bag and laughed at the old witch who had overpaid him in gold. He moved in the direction of the next house.

Galena sighed, leaning against the door. How long before her spell wore off and the collector realized he had accepted worthless pieces of metal? She hoped he wouldn't notice until he got back to the castle.

Galena was known in the area as the medicine woman. Villagers sought her out before they would turn to the leech barber. Why people felt the man was qualified to cure their ailments was beyond Galena. He could cut hair but heal the sick? Still, many put their faith in him. Neither bloodletting nor leeches cured them. It was only by luck the man hadn't killed them.

"Aunty, I am home." Biesek, her nephew, entered, taking his feathered cap, and placing it on a peg. "I saw the tax collector and feared they'd taken you." Galena harrumphed. Had the boy forgotten how powerful she was? How could he forget after she turned him into a toad? Her sister Gwendolyn sent Biesek for training a year ago when the King hunted witches in Preston. It was only a matter of time before they came to Andover knocking on her door. She and Biesek kept a low profile.

It was dangerous of Galena to trick the tax man today. Had he not been greedy, he wouldn't have seen gold coins; instead, he would have noticed the lead disks she'd put in the bag. Galena would hold off the evil ones, for as long as she could. She'd promised her sister she would protect the boy, though Biesek was hardly a boy anymore, now that he towered over her. Galena hadn't heard from her sister in weeks and was worried.

"Did you bring what I asked?" Biesek put the cloth bag on the table. Galena pulled out the contents, satisfied with the quality of the goods.

"You've done well. You are a good boy," she said, smiling.

"Aunty, I am a man, and I have proven myself to you. I am worthy to receive your knowledge." Galena thought she could not love this young man more if she had given birth to him.

"You are right. It is time." Biesek deserved to know the secrets Galena had learned from her mother, handed down from her grandmother, and now would give them to her beloved nephew.

Galena had never taught a warlock before. She sensed

Biesek's power from the beginning but decided he needed to learn discipline first. He had learned that over the past year. Great responsibility came with being a witch or warlock, as one could do irreparable harm without trying.

"Come here, nephew, let me show you our world." Biesek eagerly joined her. Galena opened some of the packages he'd purchased; being the reason they couldn't afford their taxes this time around, Galena needed to restore her potion supplies.

"We earn our living," she told him. "If we don't do our best, we won't survive. You cannot do anything that will bring suspicion on us."

"I want to work a spell, Aunty. I want to make someone do my bidding." Biesek begged; Galena frowned at her nephew, had he learned nothing in the last year? How could she put her faith in a man/child?

"You haven't listened to a word I've said. I took a great risk this morning paying Garth with lead, not gold. He will remember that I paid in gold, but if no one else gave gold, he will come back." Biesek agreed. "I am sorry that I have put us both in danger."

"Aunty, if Garth returns, I will protect you," his hand went to the small dagger at his waist. She squeezed his arm.

"That is what we try not to do, nephew. Violence only brings violence. We can protect ourselves with spells. Your first lesson will be how to protect our home. We will infuse a spell into a potion I am making now, adding the ingredients you've brought with you. By painting the doors and windows of our house, evil will not get in unless we invite it. Now shave off a few pieces of bitter root, the size of your thumb." Biesek pulled out his dagger, grateful that his aunt trusted him with her secrets.

79

"Keep us safe evermore,

Let not evil through our door.

Cast out those who dare us harm.

Keep us safe with this charm."

Galena gave her nephew a pail of the cooled potion and a brush to paint the doors and around the window frames. If Garth came back, they would be safe from him with the protection spell.

Training Biesek in her craft was Galena's dream. The lad was eager, learning quickly. She was proud of her nephew. They worked on incantations, with and without a wand. Biesek had to be able to conjure a spell on the fly.

Each night, Biesek read the tome of spells and asked her questions in the morning. They were intelligent questions.

"Aunty, I need to try my magic out so that I am prepared when the time comes." Galena agreed with him. The spell protected their home. No evil would be able to enter while they were gone. Galena still disguised the book of knowledge. If someone were to get close enough to look into the window, they would see a ferocious barking dog and not the book of spells.

"Before we begin today, we must do a spell that anything you've done will return to normal by midnight. That way, you are safe."

"Oh, great spirit, in what we delve,

returns to normal at the stroke of twelve.

Unless my nephew has done good,

then it remains, as it should."

80

She was satisfied with this spell and walked with her nephew to the village. They stood watching the butcher who was shouting at a poor woman picking through his refuse.

"Bones, I have asked for bones to make soup for my children. You would throw them out anyway." The woman begged sadly

"Beggar, be gone!"

"Aunty, why wouldn't the man give that woman scrap bones to feed starving children?"

"Greed, simple greed." She waited to see what Biesek would do. He wiggled his fingers at the butcher.

"Bones to boil for soup you'll give,

you greedy little man.

A meal where hungry children live,

given by your hand."

"Wait!" the butcher recanted. "Take these bones. I would throw them out anyway." The grateful mother picked from the scrap pile. Galena smiled, knowing Biesek understood his gift and would use it wisely. Upon seeing Garth, the tax collector, Galena shrunk behind her nephew.

"Biesek, we must leave, now!" Garth stopped at each door on his rounds, this was not tax day, yet he was collecting. Taking his aunt's arm, Biesek and Galena hurried home.

"Do we have enough this time?" Biesek emptied the small box containing their earnings. Galena knew they wouldn't have enough because the King asked for more each time. It was impossible to meet his demands.

Fire, she smelled the smoke. No doubt someone wasn't able to pay, and the cruel Garth lit their home on fire.

"Nephew, we must hide the book in the woods. The spell on our house keeps evil from coming in, but Garth could set our home on fire. We must protect it at all costs. Biesek wrapped the heavy book in a tablecloth escaping into the woods. When he returned, they waited for Garth and the soldiers.

"Do you think the spell will hold?" Biesek looked out the window anxiously. Galena had no comforting words for him. for she now suspected the fate of her sister Gwendolyn and was saddened by it.

The soldiers tried to walk the path to the cottage. Their feet sank into muck. The brush that had grown around the house did not allow them to leave the path.

"Aunty, look," Biesek clapped his hands. "The spell is working." As the men tried to move toward the cottage, they sunk deeper into quicksand. If they retreated, they stood on solid ground again. Biesek walked out the door and tossed a sack of coins to Garth.

"Since we've had all that rain, we haven't been able to leave here." Garth caught the bag and moved on with his men.

"What did you give him?" Galena asked her nephew suspiciously.

"Gold."

"We have no gold."

"But we do. I put a spell on my money pouch. We have money anytime we need it."

"Oh, Biesek, what have you done?"

"Something I am surprised you never thought of." Galena was horrified,

"There is a reason I never did that. It is forbidden. It's one thing to make Garth think he received gold coins because his greed made him see what he wanted. It is another, benefitting yourself with unlimited funds. It's against our code, and you will suffer every time that gold changes hands." Galena took the magic bag and threw it into the fire.

"What kinds of things will happen to me?" Biesek asked her.

"I don't know. It depends on what the money is used for."

After months had gone by without anything terrible happening, Biesek was convinced his aunt was wrong. He no longer feared the consequences of what he'd done. Things were going so well that together, he and his aunt had been able to support themselves and pay their tax but had not heard from his mother. Biesek hired a carriage to take them to his boyhood home in Preston.

Gone.

All that was left was the blackened wood where his home once stood. They searched through the rubble and found nothing. Biesek asked the carriage driver to stop at the neighbor's home.

"Biesek," the elderly man came from the cottage embracing him.

"Where is my mother? What happened to our home?" The man shook his head sadly.

"Months ago, the King's men came to collect. Your mother didn't have enough. So, they set your house on fire."

83

Biesek was inconsolable. Galena wept with him. They would return to Andover without Gwendolyn.

On the journey home, the driver pulled to the side of the road to rest. Biesek and Galena walked around to stretch their legs when Biesek spied a giant toad. Deciding the fat toad could be used for some spell, Biesek picked it up, putting it in his satchel.

They arrived late that evening at the cottage. Once inside, the toad raised a ruckus.

"What is that noise?" Galena asked.

"It's a large toad I found on our way back from Preston." Biesek pulled the toad from his bag, setting it on the table, where it sat calmly, blinking.

"Biesek, that is not an average toad. That is an enchanted person." Excitedly, Galena opened the spellbook turning several pages; she scrolled with her finger to find a reversing spell.

"Oh bewitched, beguiled, and sold

Turn yourself back from a croaking toad." Galena threw her magic dust in a poof of smoke that wafted in the air, but the toad remained on the table.

"This is powerful magic." Galena walked in a circle around the table. "Biesek, hold my hands. We shall do a double spell, using both of our magic. They clasped hands over the toad.

"Magic fills this our abode.

Change back human from a toad." The poof of smoke.

"Mother!" Biesek cried. Galena hugged her sister Gwendolyn who sat on the table where the toad had been.

"How did you become a toad?" Galena asked her sister.

"When they lit my house on fire, I turned myself into a

toad and burrowed deep underground. I was making my way to Andover when I called for your driver to stop. I was lucky that it was Biesek who picked me up. I knew that you, sister, would recognize me as an enchanted creature." Biesek and Galena were overjoyed.

When Garth returned, he claimed they owed more, seeing they had added an extra room to the house. With three of them working, they were able to pay.

A great drought dried up everything around them; there had been no rain for months. The King could not collect taxes from those who had nothing. Biesek, Gwendolyn, and Galena had a lush garden sharing their bounty with neighbors, but soon word got out about them.

"Witch! Come out!" Garth called from the front of the house, "Come out, or we shall burn you out." Gwendolyn opened the door.

"No!" Galena shouted as her sister walked toward Garth. Biesek tried to grab his mother, but she threw her energy at him dashing him to the floor.

"Mother!" he shouted as Gwendolyn allowed the men to take her away. Her punishment for escaping them in Preston.

"Aunty, we have to go after her!"

"We need a plan," Galena assured her nephew they could rescue Gwendolyn.

Galena walked by the castle, placing a large toad on the ground before the gates. The toad hopped past the guards who didn't notice it, and then it swam across the moat, where it found a waste pipe that led out of the dungeon.

The bewitched toad hopped along until he found his mother in a cell then came close to the snoring guard as leaned lazily against the wall. The giant toad stood on its hind legs, removing the key from a spike next to the sleeping guard.

Gwendolyn opened the cell with the key the toad presented, she knew it was Biesek when she touched him and was transformed into a toad herself. Together, they left the dungeon through the pipe and returned to the gate. Galena picked them up and carried them away.

At a safe distance from the castle, she restored mother and son. The three of them were jubilant until Biesek collapsed.

"Biesek!" Gwendolyn rushed to her son's side. Biesek's eyes rolled back into his head. Galena knew the King had spent the ill-gotten gold. It most likely had been stored away this last many months, but the King was forced to dip into his treasure due to the drought. Someone was ill. That was why Biesek had fallen sick. She needed to find out what was going on.

Galena put her hands on Biesek's head. Seeing the problem, she turned into a crow flying off to search for the gold that Biesek made from the magic pouch.

The castle windows draped in black, the King's daughter near death, and King Ferd paid the leech barber to save his daughter. Galena flew through the window, landing on the princess' bed.

"It's an omen of ill will," cried the King. Galena transformed into her true self.

"Witch!" cried the barber.

"You charlatan, pretending to heal the sick for the King's treasure." The barber dropped his bag of gold and ran off. Galena picked it up, giving it back to the King after she removed the ill-gotten coins. She held them in her hand.

"This is my fee." The King nodded in agreement. Galena

removed the leeches from the girl's body, offering the gold to the spirits who protected her.

"Oh, great spirit if you please,

heal our Princess, Ann Louise.

Ill-gotten gold I give in lieu,

please save her life, I beg of you."

The black drapes fell from the windows, and the wind of ill will sailed out of the room

The Princess stirred in her bed, and her eyes fluttered open. The King ran to her embracing his daughter.

"Anything you ask," he said to Galena.

"Sire. I ask that you leave my family be. We mean no harm, and I will always be here for you." The King pulled off his pinky ring and gave it to her.

"You have my word." Galena transformed into a crow with the ruby ring in her beak. She flew through the window.

Gwendolyn sat on the ground next to Biesek, who seemed to have come out of the spell.

"What happened?" he asked. Galena gave her nephew the King's ring.

"The ill-gotten gold nearly killed you, but I have given it back. You are safe from the curse. Let's go home."

Gwendolyn snapped her fingers. A farmer in a wagon came around the corner stopping before them.

"Do ye need a ride?" They climbed into the back of the wagon, and the farmer took them to their cottage.

"I hear that a witch lives here, be careful." He slapped the reins on the horse's back, and the animal pulled the wagon away. The three looked at one another with knowing smiles and laughed.

"A curse upon this house I lift.

Free from harm because this gift."

Biesek canted holding the ring toward their home. The thick overgrowth peeled away; the quicksand disappeared.

As they stepped into the cottage, lightning flashed across the sky, and thunder rolled.

"Biesek," Galena warned.

"I did nothing, Aunty; the drought is over."

Dawn DeBraal

Dawn DeBraal lives in rural Wisconsin with her husband Red, two rescue dogs, and a stray cat. She has published well over 400 short stories, poems and drabbles in online magazines and anthologies. Her love of telling a good story can also be written. https://linktr.ee/dawndebraal

Flying
By: James Dorr

THE FEEL OF a rake handle between my thighs. Or a distaff, or broomstick. It does not matter. It is the *flying* — the feel of release as a bird that takes to the air. The feel of the wind, the billow of skirts, the sun beating down or the moon above me. A kestrel. A corbie. A night bird. An owl. And so, I too, fly as a bird beneath the sky.

So it is, so it was, but it was not always. Once a maiden, I lived as other maids.

Born of a family of some status in Granada, I grew up a beauty, or so they told me. My hair long and lustrous, my form straight but not too tall.

And my eyes, blue, the right one, especially, as blue as the sea on a summer's day.

#

And so, they sent for me, the King's Court at Madrid, to be

a Lady in Waiting to the King's new bride, the Duchess Elizabeth of Parma. Or so they told me.

My family, of course, bade me goodbye swiftly. "An honor," they told me. "Go in God, Juana," my father said to me. "Remember, every day, your devotions," my mother added, though neither he nor she would look me in the eye as they said these words. Rather they packed me things, herbs and ointments, helped with my clothing, fixed me a basket of dates and oranges so I could have sweets to eat on my journey.

Thus, I came north up through Andalusia, climbing above the Sierra Morena to the vast *meseta*, where wind and sky battle with each other freely, and there are two seasons — two seasons only throughout the whole year — or so the Castilians say. Hell, and winter.

And it was winter.

I crossed the Tagus, staying the night with those who conveyed me in brooding Toledo, then threaded my way up the Rio Jarama. I came to Madrid itself, then to the castle beyond the city, a sprawling structure beneath the Sierra de Guadarrama, with high walls and towers that surrounded gardens yet failed to keep out the wind. Everywhere within the castle I found clocks — I found out later that these were the playthings of Charles, the Emperor, who died one hundred and fifty years before when the king's palace was still at Toledo, and yet, because they were his, had been brought here. I met the new queen, and the palace dwarfs — everywhere one turned, one found dwarfs spying — and I met the *Cardenal*, Giulio Alberoni, that she had brought with her. And learned to avoid him.

I learned my duties.

#

You see, I knew how to heal. That was a skill I had learned in Granada. That, yes, and other things, which I learned later. I finally met the king, Philip V, the Bourbon monarch who had come to the throne after the bloody Wars of the Succession, and found him in his bed, a melancholic. Later, I found, he would lie there for months on end, scarcely shaving or changing his stinking shirts, leaving the palace's care to his bride and her priests and her minions.

And, always, the wind blew free, the creeping wind of the *meseta* — the high plateau. This was the wind that had killed the Emperor, so the Castilians claimed, himself the conqueror of half of Europe, and yet was so subtle it would not extinguish the flame of a candle that burned at his bedside. This was the wind that ruffled women's skirts, that sickened and brought to death yet more kings afterward, even after the move to this castle where it had been hoped the air might be more healthful. This was the wind that rustled through corridors, chilling the stone, that rattled the roof tiles and blew smoke down chimneys.

I came to adore the wind, standing alone at the top of a tower. If, outside, it was the season of winter, then inside the castle it surely was Hell.

Mornings, when not looking to the king's sickness, I wound the clocks. That was my duty too. These were the clocks that were placed too high for the queen's dwarfs to reach. And yet they could reach *me*, prodding me, pinching me. Pulling me down to them.

When I complained, the king's bride laughed out loud. "Best you wear more petticoats, my dear," she said. And so, I *did* wear more, little that it helped me.

Nor was the *Cardenal* Alberoni nor his priests any help to me either. They hated me, every one. Alberoni, my very

93

first day, took me aside and hissed in my face, "I know you woman." He wouldn't look in my eye. "I know you, *strega*," he said. "You are evil. My priests will be watching."

He would not confess me when I needed solace, nor would his priests, nor would even our own Spanish priests who also lived within the palace. And so, I climbed up the walls at night to the highest tower and spoke to the wind. *Mi viento.* I told it my troubles.

I told it of the king. How he grew worse sometimes. Sometimes better. How, sometimes, he grabbed me too. I told it of his wife and how she let her dwarfs run rampant, throwing food — and worse! — rutting in hallways, attacking the serving maids. Showing no trace of morality or restraint.

I took, myself, to wearing a dagger within my bodice — I told the wind this too.

I told it about the clocks. About their ticking. About how the queen would scratch at my face and eyes if she found even one a second slow. And others would pull my hair when I then reached up to try to adjust it.

And how the king didn't care. How the priests — priests of God, except I knew now that there was no God, at least not as the priests taught — would stand about laughing when I wept my sorrows.

And some would do more than laugh.

This all I told the wind. And sometimes, at God's will — God's or the Devil's, it does not matter — the wind would answer.

#

You see, I had learned well that there was no God. No God of goodness, as the priests taught of. Rather, there were Gods of the castle, of rumor and scandal, lies and backbiting. There were the Gods of the dwarfs and their sundry lusts — and the lusts of the larger people also. The God of sickness who, sometimes, I held at bay, just long enough for the king to be lucid sufficiently for the queen to go in to him. The God of the priests and the Inquisition — oh yes, that, too, had reached into the palace — and of the *cardenal* and of Rome.

The God of the wind above and of the winter sky.

And the wind answered, telling me to be free.

#

So it went, one season, two seasons, until the year came at last back full circle. So, it repeated, again, another year, the seasons circling like hawks in the bleak sky. And life in the castle, it circled also, circles within circles, clocks always turning. The clocks' hands circling within other hands' expanse.

I *never* loved the king. Yet gossip circled, too, within the palace. I did, after all, spend much time with him.

It was my duty.

And when he grew worse, ah, the priests watched more closely, whispering to the queen. The dwarfs grew bolder.

And my health, too, faded, or seemed at first to fade, yet, when I stood alone on the battlements speaking out to the wind, *inside* I grew strong. I looked in the mirror I had in my chamber and saw how my eyes, so strangely blue for one from Granada, grew light with the seasons until the left one — my left eye especially! — became as pale and as hard

95

as the winter sky.

And on the inside, oh yes, I grew hard too. I had needs, of course, my soul *and* my body. My health and my duty — my hands grew powerful from winding the palace clocks. My skills grew more subtle as I ministered to the king's bedside.

Yet, despite rumor, I never loved him.

But I did have needs too, the same as the queen did. The same as all women. I spoke to the wind of these, and I was answered. And, as I know now, there were others who listened.

The priests, you see, dressed in gray, blending with stone as they crept through the castle on soundless feet. What they heard they compared to what they later would hear in Confession. Except in my case, of course — they called me *infiel*, one not of their Faith and thus not allowed even that small comfort that comes with contrition.

But they would hear others, and thus, on the words of others, condemn me.

I never loved the king, but I had needs, too. Needs and desires. And there was Alvarez, the chief of the queen's dwarfs, a man who the Gods in their mirth had made large in one part of his body as if to compensate for his minuteness in all of the others. Alvarez, who came from the south as I did — who taught me much of myself and my origins. Things I had not known.

And so, they condemned me, the Roman priests first, then the Spanish priests of the Inquisition. The *cardenal* helped them in their labors, stripping the clothes from me to search for birthmarks. Smiling and whispering to me about the king, since that had been the pretext for their questionings, though even he knew I had never loved Philip.

Yet throughout it all, no one would dare to mention the name of the queen's dwarf, Alvarez, who was my true downfall. Because the queen loved him too.

#

Oh yes, I knew that. I spoke to the wind, by then on a more than daily basis. Even when locked in my cell, cut off from the sky, I spoke to it through the narrow window.

And, always now, it answered. It was the wind that had warned me to be strong when Giulio Alberoni stripped the clothes from me and probed with his fingers searching for blemishes on my body. At last, he said, "Yes! You see, here, in the cleft between her buttocks. The red of the witch-mark."

I felt his fingers pinch, yet it was not needed. The mark was there, in the shape of a mouse — I knew because Alvarez had told me — even without his probing and pinching. And the other too, that which had branded me even as I had set foot in the palace that first winter day, the mark of my eyes. My strange blue eyes, for a southern woman.

"*Si! Fascinatrix*," the *Cardenal* Giulio Alberoni had whispered to his priests on the very first day he had seen me. "The strange blue eyes, of uneven color. The pale, left one evil."

The others repeated it, switching from his Italian to Spanish.

"*Mal de ojo!*"

"The eye of the *bruja!*"

And yet I would not confess, even with torture. Rather I

wheedled, I cajoled the *cardenal*, pressing my naked body against his chest. "Look in my eye," I said. "See of its wonders. Does it fascinate *you?"*

Others would turn and look despite Alberoni's warnings and scream and faint as my eye blazed blue at them. I heard more screams late at night, those of those same priests at their flagellations, atoning for weakness. For they had gazed at me, and that in itself was sin.

And I laughed at them at last, on the eighth day of my inquisition. Laughed when the *cardenal*, weary, turned toward me, and could not resist a glance.

Laughed when I spat on him, then even louder when they bound my arms and carried me outside.

#

The stake was waiting — it was as it should be. As it would be always.

I looked at the queen above, on her balcony, gazing downward, and laughed when she turned away. Laughed when, above *her*, an owl flew in daylight.

I make no apology.

Always, the wind above — I pushed the cross away when a younger priest, one more compassionate than the others, dared hold it up to me — and raised my face to the sky so pale and hard, yet deep and beautiful, much like my own eye. The one they avoided, still, as they set the wood at my feet ablaze. Yet in the sky itself, always above them, the same blue paleness was spiraling with the wind. Circling with the smoke that rose around me.

The updraft lifting me! A rake! A broomstick! I flew with

the heat, a whirlwind of ashes. A kestrel! A corbie!

Knowing now what I know of Gods and Devils, of dwarfs and of queens — "*The fools!*" *I cried out as I circled higher* — and of *cardenales* and poor, mad monarchs —

Of night birds!

Of eagles!

That it is the wind and the sky and the *flame* that set the spirit of a witch free.

THE END

James Dorr

Indiana writer James Dorr's The Tears of Isis was a 2013 Bram Stoker Award® finalist for Fiction Collection, with his latest, Tombs: A Chronicle of Latter-Day Times of Earth, a novel-in-stories from Elder Signs Press. He has previously worked as a technical writer, an editor on a regional magazine, a full time non-fiction freelancer, and a semi-professional musician, and currently harbors a Goth cat named Triana. Readers may also visit Dorr's blog at http://jamesdorrwriter.wordpress.com

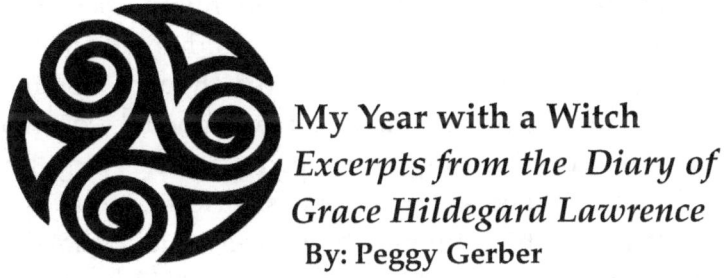

My Year with a Witch
Excerpts from the Diary of
Grace Hildegard Lawrence
By: Peggy Gerber

DEAR DIARY,

Screw you! The last thing I want to do is write down my problems in a diary and re-live the event, but my therapist said if I don't start doing my assignments, I will never get better. She made my mother cry. So here it is. My name is Gracie, I am nineteen years old, and I can't leave the house. I spend my days sitting in my room, eating cereal straight from the box and binge-watching reality tv. My diagnosis is agoraphobia, PTSD, anxiety, depression, and survivor's guilt. Since it is just Mom and me, Mom decided I would go next door to Hildy's house everyday while she was at work. I told her I could stay alone, I feel so stupid going to a babysitter, but she insisted. So, starting tomorrow, Mom will walk me to Hildy's house early in the morning and I will spend the day there. Don't get me wrong, I like Hildy, I just don't want to hang out with a middle-aged woman all day. Plus, I am pretty sure Hildy is a witch.

Dear Diary,

When I walked into Hildy's living room my eyes almost popped out of my head: there were acrylic bowls filled with beads everywhere. Her house was like an obstacle course. I couldn't believe this is where my mother wanted me to spend my days. I sort of knew Hildy made and sold jewelry on her website, but I never thought about the process. After I grunted hello, I sat down on the couch and rolled a few beads in my hands as I watched Hildy finish off a bracelet. When she was done, she closed her eyes and mumbled something unintelligible over it. It sounded like an incantation, so I asked her straight out, "Hildy, are you a witch?" She laughed and answered, "I am not a witch, Gracie. It's just a simple prayer." Out of curiosity, I took out my phone and googled her website. Her product description claimed her jewelry would bring good luck, and she had like a gazillion five-star reviews. I was skeptical, of course, but not stupid, so I asked her to make something for me. I could really use some luck.

Dear Diary,

A sliver of hope has crept back into my life. I was able to walk around the block all by myself without having a panic attack. I know how lame that sounds, but I actually cried. I suspect it has something to do with the necklace Hildy made for me. It's really pretty. Hildy let me pick out all my favorite beads and then she strung them together adding on a crystal vial filled with this blue-green luminescent liquid. It is a real statement piece. As I was taking my walk, the crystal shimmered in the sunlight almost as if it were a diamond and I was so mesmerized I forgot to panic. Hildy said the liquid will evaporate little by little, and when it is all gone, I'll know I'm completely better. I gave a cynical snort and asked again, "Are you a witch? Hildy chuckled and said, " I am not a witch, Gracie." When I told my therapist about my little success, she said it was due to the therapy, and that I am actually doing my homework now. She also said the medication was finally kicking in. Little does she know I stopped taking my medicine weeks ago. It was making me fat and I didn't need one more reason to hate myself.

Dear Diary,

I had a set-back today. I went to the supermarket and as I was checking out a truck backfired and threw me into a full-blown panic. I began hyperventilating and felt like I was having a heart attack. I dropped my basket on the floor and raced straight back to Hildy's house. By the time I got there, I was sobbing uncontrollably. She took me in her arms and rubbed my back, just like my grandma used to do. I felt like such a failure, but Hildy said she was proud of me for for trying. Then she pointed out that some of the liquid in the crystal had evaporated. I can't believe she got me to smile on such a bad day.

Dear Diary,

Today Hildy had to go out to pick up some supplies. She asked if I wanted to come, but I told her I needed to practice staying home alone. That was a lie. I had been coming to her house for six weeks already and I wasn't going to pass up this opportunity to snoop around and find out once and for all of she was a witch. As soon as she left, I raced upstairs, and her bedroom door creaked open on its own like it was expecting me. I slowly crept inside and pumped my fist in the air shouting, "Yes, I knew it." There, on her shelves were hundreds of bottles of potions in every color of the rainbow. I started walking around the room, touching all the bottles until I got to her night table and almost threw up. She had a giant jar of eyeballs floating in formaldehyde. I know what it smells like because we dissected frogs in high school biology. As I pinched my nose in disgust, there was another surprise. A parrot flew out nowhere and started chirping, "Gracie is a bad girl. Gracie is a bad girl." I ran out of the room and blasted my music until Hildy returned. When she walked in, I pointed at her and said, "You are a witch." She winked, put a finger to her lips and said, "Shhh. Our little secret."

Dear Diary,

Now that the parrot is no longer a secret, Hildy lets him fly freely around the house. It turns out the parrot can talk. Like really talk. I asked him his name and he told me it was Stanley Rostakowski. I wrinkled my brow and asked, "Hildy, you named your parrot Stanley Rostakowski?" She snapped, "I didn't name him that, his mother did." Out of curiosity I pulled out my phone and googled the name and it turns out it's the same name as Hildy's second husband. There was a police report that said he has been missing for twelve years. I bellowed, "Hildy, you turned your husband into a parrot!" She barked back, "Gracie, husbands should not cheat on their wives," then chucked a bead at Stanley's head.

Dear Diary,

Another huge step. I went to my first support group today. It was over Zoom. There were six other messed up kids in the group and when it was my turn to speak, everything came pouring out. The gunshots, the terror, the blood, and the whole aftermath. So here it is dear diary, I had been sitting in the college library doing some research, when a student came in with a gun and started shooting. All the kids jumped under tables or ran outside, but I was too petrified to move. I just sat there like a statue. My biology teacher spotted me and screamed for me to duck, but I couldn't, so he jumped over the table and shoved me underneath. And then he was shot. Three people died that day, and one of them was because of me.

Dear Diary,

The day after support group, one third of the blue liquid from my necklace was gone. I think talking about the event lifted a weight off my shoulders. I feel like I am finally getting better. I was so happy I called my friend Rachel and arranged to meet her for coffee. I know she is still mad at me for ignoring all her calls and texts. I hope she'll forgive me. The coffee shop is ten blocks away and I am going there myself. I will rub my necklace for good luck.

Dear Diary,

I got a job! Well, sort of. I've been asking Hildy for months if I can help her make jewelry and she finally said yes. I am thankful because now I can help Mom pay some of my medical expenses. I still see my therapist once a week, and Mom had to take a second job to pay the psychiatrist. The hardest part of making the jewelry is getting the incantation right. It sounds like gibberish, so I had to learn it phonetically. In other good news, I am going on a date with Ben from support group. He's really shy so I was the one that asked him out. I was so nervous to ask him, but he said yes right away like he didn't have to think about it. Afterwards I called Rachel to tell her, and she said she was worried about me going out with a boy who has a mental illness. Then I reminded her that I have one too. It will be really nice hanging out with someone that I don't have to hide things from.

Dear Diary,

I have fallen into a very comfortable routine. Each morning I go to Hildy's, and we spend the day together making jewelry and chatting. Stanley likes to join in, but sometimes he says inappropriate things and I have to shoo him away. I've actually become very artistic and Hildy says she's proud of some of my unique creations. I love chatting with Hildy, she is really insightful, I wonder if that is a witch thing. When I talk about the event with my therapist, she tells me it wasn't my fault. That it was my biology teacher's choice to save me. That I have nothing to feel guilty about. Hildy gets me. She doesn't try to convince me that I had no part in it. She told me when my teacher died, my world became lopsided, and that one day I will save someone, and my world will straighten out.

Dear Diary,

This morning Mom burst into tears when she couldn't get her car started. I am really worried about her; all she ever does is work and worry about me. I knocked on Hildy's door and she came with a green potion hidden behind her back. Just as mom was pulling out her phone to call AAA, Hildy poured the potion into the engine and the car started. Mom gave a huge sigh of relief and invited Hildy for dinner. Then she whispered in my ear, "There is something very strange about that woman." I just smiled.

Dear Diary,

Ben and I celebrated our three-month anniversary last

night at Ye Old Ice Cream Shoppe. We ordered a gigantic three scoop sundae with whipped cream and four cherries. After a few spoonfuls, Ben lowered his head, put his spoon down and whispered he had something to tell me. He confessed that the night I asked him out, he was feeling so hopeless he planned to commit suicide. Tears came to my eyes, and I put my arms around him and impulsively blurted out that I loved him. As soon as I said that my heart began to race because I never said that to any boy before. Then I realized I really meant it. Ben started crying and said he loved me too. He never thought he could be happy again. We spent the next few hours eating ice cream, holding hands, and talking. He swore he would get help if he ever had those bad thoughts again. When I got home, I took off my necklace and noticed three quarters of the liquid had evaporated. Hildy was right. My world was straightening out. When I told Hildy I saved a life she said, "Great. Now go save another."

Dear Diary,

Mom and I talked it over and we agreed I am ready to start college again. Not in person, of course, I'm not that crazy. I've decided to study entomology. Just kidding, I want to become a psychologist that specializes in PTSD and survivor's guilt. I can do all my undergraduate work at home, and I'll get my PhD in person. Imagine that Dr. Grace Ann Lawrence. I might write a book.

Dear Diary,

It's been four months since my last panic attack, and almost nine months since this whole nightmare began. College is going well, and Ben and I are still dating. His dad is in rehab for a while, so he is staying with me and Mom, in separate rooms of course. I continue to go to Hildy's house every day. It's a routine that I still need, and Hildy has begun teaching me some spells. I think Mom is a little jealous that I go there so much, but I enjoy being with Hildy and I've even grown to like the company of Stanley Rostakowski.

Dear Diary,

Even though it's been about a year now since the event, and I feel back to normal, my necklace still has some of the blue liquid in it. I asked Hildy why she couldn't just zap me and make me completely better, but she said she can't undo what happened. It will always be a part of me. That I will do great things with my life, but I will always be vulnerable and will have to work hard to keep myself mentally healthy. She also said the necklace played no part in my healing. That it was all me. That I should be proud of myself. I am.

Dear Diary,

I think I'm cursed. I'd been nagging Mom to go to the doctor for weeks and she finally did. The doctor ordered a bunch of tests and diagnosed her with lung cancer. When she told me I felt like a bomb had exploded in my brain. I ran straight to Hildy's and pounded on her door screaming her name. I wobbled into her house on jelly legs and fell into her arms hysterically crying. She immediately noticed that the crystal of my necklace was completely full of blue liquid again, and knew it was bad. I told her about Mom and dropped to my knees and begged Hildy to save her. To do whatever it took. Hildy remained calm, put her hands on my shoulders and said, "Gracie get up. Of course, I'll help you. Just give me twenty-four hours to take care of a few things first." I went home shaking but feeling well enough to cook dinner for me and Mom. Afterwards, we watched a movie.

Dear Diary,

I paced back and forth all day, barely able to breathe until Hildy arrived. I brought her straight into Mom's bedroom and gasped when she pulled out a knife. Mom began whimpering but I told her to trust Hildy and do whatever she said. Hildy began a low chant as she made cuts on both Mom's hands and then did the same to her own. She took Mom's hands into hers and as their blood flowed together Hildy chanted one of her incantations. Her eyes were closed, and her body swayed back and forth as her chanting grew louder and louder. When she was done, she laid down on the bed next to Mom and said she needed to rest. As I bent down to thank her, my eyes popped open as I watched her raven black hair turn white and her skin begin to wrinkle and become translucent. I screamed, "Hildy, what's happening?" She told me she gave my mother thirty more healthy years. She took it from her own life. I started shrieking "No! You can't do this." I begged her to regenerate. She smiled her last smile and told me that she was a witch, not Doctor Who and that she was happy to do this for us. She said she was already one hundred-twenty years old and that was enough life for anyone. Then her body combusted and the little that remained flew up into the air like burning embers. She was gone.

Dear Diary,

Thank you for being such a good friend. It's been a year since Hildy's death, and I miss her terribly. She left her house and most of her belongings to her great-grandchildren, but she left the business and her potions to me. She also left Stanley to me, but first put a spell on him so he can't talk anymore. He likes to sit on my mom's lap. It is a little creepy. For now, I am working towards my PhD and Mom runs the business from our home. She loves it. She still does not understand what happened, but it is wonderful to see her happy again. I noticed she does the incantations perfectly and the jewelry continues to bring people good luck. I think Hildy transferred a little witch into her when they mixed blood. Ben is doing very well too. He is in nursing school to become a psychiatric nurse and now he is the facilitator of support group. I am so proud of him. Oh, and we got engaged on my twenty-first birthday. Don't worry, we won't get married until we both graduate. Meanwhile, I changed my middle name to Hildegard in honor of Hildy and her selfless sacrifice. I will always cherish my year with the witch. The best/worst year of my life.

Peggy Gerber

Peggy Gerber is a poet and short story writer from Northern New Jersey. Her works have appeared in many publications including The World of Myth Magazine, Daily Science Fiction, Everyday Fiction, Potato Soup Journal and many others. She is thrilled to be one of the finalists in the Open Contract Challenge and looks forward to publication of her first poetry chapbook, Stumbling in CrazyTown.

The Woman of Red
(*La Mujer de Rojo*)
By: Stephen Johnson

ISABELLE STROLLED LEISURELY along the rocky shoreline wrapping her arms around her chest while pulling the sweater sleeves over her hands. The cool breeze blew in as the sun fought to peek through the gray clouds overhead. A cold gust blew a froth of seawater up across the rocks and the mist hit her face as she screamed out in surprise. "Just perfect," she smirked as she turned to leave and go back to her car. A day that started out with such promise of a warm sunny day had quickly turned into a foreboding and brooding Saturday morning in the small Rhode Island town.

Isabelle stepped cautiously over the chipped rocks and uneven pebbles that covered the shore but stopped as she noticed a bright piece of stone. She routinely visited this beach in hopes of finding rare and unique sea glass for her jewelry collection but had given up with that endeavor this morning. That is until she spotted the ornate beautiful pieces sitting further up the rocky shore. "Wow," she exclaimed without thinking, *usually don't find pieces this far inland from the water.* She bent over to examine the small pieces of chipped glass and noticed that it was actually a collection of a larger piece that must have stayed close together.

Strange, never found pieces like this. There were five pieces of glass forming a perfect circle on the ground. They were unique and beautiful enough, each one perfectly cut and shaped to resemble each other almost like it was designed. The bright ruby color had smooth edges, and as she picked up one a ray of sunlight caught her hand illuminating the piece displaying its true beauty. Isabelle looked down again past the circle of the five ruby red pieces at the centerpiece. In the middle of the stone circle sat a slightly larger piece. It resembled the shape of its smaller sisters but carried a darker red hue that set it apart from the others. Isabelle knelt down and picked up the six pieces, smiling at the find as she placed them in her special pouch. With an impatient and excited pace, she nearly ran to the car already dreaming up the jewelry she would create tonight.

Later that night, Isabelle sat perched over the center dark red stone peering down through the magnifying glass attached to her right eye. Carefully, she placed the drill into the center of the glass, careful to not damage the surrounding areas. The small drill began its work and the familiar smell of the burning friction drifted up as she concentrated staring down into the piece of glass. After a few minutes, she lifted the drill to observe the progress and noticed the sea glass remained unscathed.

"Looks like you are going to be difficult," she whispered as she set her enhanced drill bit in place for this job.

This time the drill penetrated the small sea glass, and she felt the drill bit carve into the middle of the piece. She noticed a dark stain through the magnifying glass and suddenly felt a sharp pain in the side of her head. The pain was so intense that she had to stop drilling for a moment. She rubbed her forehead gently for a few seconds before reengaging on the small ruby stone. Isabelle placed the drill bit carefully in the small groove that was started previously and finished the small hole this time without incident.

After finishing the main ruby sea glass stone, Isabelle quickly completed the drilling on the remaining five pieces. She stretched as she straightened in her seat, trying to rid herself of the kink in her back. She glanced over to the clock mid stretch and exhaled a long yawn. *Three in the morning, no wonder I feel tired. Time must have got away from me.* Isabelle set the equipment aside and secured the power to the drill before getting ready for bed.

That night, sleep came quickly for her. Isabelle tossed in the bed as she dreamed of a ship thrown about as waves crashed against the sides of the hull. She felt the violent rocking as she looked out from the deck of the old sailing ship and could feel the heavy rain from the storm as it pelted the side of her face. Confused she found a ladder well leading down from the main deck. She stumbled down the old wooden ladder out of the rain and found herself in a small passageway. The wind howled from the opening above like a wolf crying out in the night, but she was at least now out of the biting cold rain from above. Voices reached her from a space a few feet down the old ship's passageway. She walked slowly noticing a cabin and the door slightly ajar.

Isabelle peeked into the small room trying to brace herself as the ship pitched wildly. Inside the room she could see a group of men fighting. She looked closer and noticed four of the men desperately trying to hold one of the other men down. Around the room, several others lay bloodied and still. The man being held to the ground burst up from the floor and with what seemed the strength of ten men threw the remaining occupants of the room off. With dizzying speed, he produced a sword and with a bloodthirsty scream, he finished the work he had started with the remaining four men in the room.

Isabelle backed up in shock as the man looked up towards the door. His eyes met hers and she could still see the rage in his face and the loss of control he displayed. She began to turn when the man's attention diverted back to a table in the middle of the room. A beautiful gold chalice sat on the table adorned with various small jewels but by far the most distinguishable piece of the cup sat embedded in the side. A brilliant ruby stone set into the side of the chalice burned a strange dark red glow as the man feverishly grabbed the cup with both hands. He murmured incoherently the same phrase over and over as Isabelle tried to listen to his words. "Mi amor, mi vida por ella."

A large wave hit the starboard side and Isabelle was thrown into the bulkhead momentarily bringing the man out of his trance. He focused back on her and moved toward the door holding the chalice with a death grip and screaming at Isabelle, "It is mine! La mujer de rojo es mia! The Woman of Red is mine! My life for her."

With a sudden look towards her that belayed recognition, he broke off enthusiastically toward her. "My love, my love!" He reached toward Isabelle longingly. Isabelle backed from the door and fell as he burst into the passageway.

Isabelle shot up straight in her bed as the alarm clock blared to her right. She took in deep breaths as she threw the sweat-stained sheets off and slid to the head of the bed frame curling her legs under her arms. After a few minutes, her breathing relaxed and she felt her body calm down. She even let out a small laugh as she realized it was all just a dream, a very vivid dream.

Isabelle relaxed and got out of bed as she noticed it was almost eight o'clock in the morning. Cursing herself, she jumped in the shower to get ready for work. "I can't believe I overslept! I am so late!" She stammered out loud throwing out her clothes to get ready as quickly as possible.

Later that night, Isabelle returned home after an uneventful day at work and immediately returned to her workshop. Her thoughts all day remained on the strange but beautiful sea glass. Completely absorbed by the six ruby pieces, she saw her creation in her head. She would create her masterpiece, a beautiful gold necklace with the sea glass stones hanging from separate smaller gold chains. The centerpiece of the massive necklace would be the large dark ruby piece. Isabelle unlocked the small safe from under her workshop to find the gold chain she kept secured. Very rarely used, but on this occasion, she was glad she saved it.

Completely obsessed with her masterpiece, Isabelle worked relentlessly through the afternoon and into the night. Her stomach rumbled, but she ignored its calls. She proceeded slowly with painstaking attention to detail as she assembled the necklace. Finally, after her body could no longer continue what her mind commanded, she laid her head down on the work desk. *I will just rest for a moment,* she told herself. Completely exhausted, she set her head down and closed her eyes.

Tonight, the dreams reached Isabelle again only she found herself standing outside a small dark cave. A faint light reached into the cave, and she noticed etchings on the entrance. Strange symbols marked the outside of the cave that she had never seen. She shivered as she passed through the entrance and looked closer at one of the markings, "Is that dried blood?"

She walked slowly down the cavern toward the light that

117

appeared brighter and radiated heat outward the closer she moved into the cave. Fire embers flowed out and burned her lungs as the cavern's passageway narrowed and she found herself deep within the cave. As on the ship, she could hear voices talking up ahead yet this time, there was no fighting. She could make out at least two female voices talking.

She could hear one of the women reciting something that sounded Latin over and over. The other woman began chanting. Isabelle peeked around to see a group of five women sitting around a large square block. A large red ruby shining brilliantly sat in the middle of the block surrounded by a circle of fire that burned surrounding he whole structure. Another woman raised her arms up and then picked up a large ancient scroll as she began talking.

"Since the dawn of the Woman of Red,

We have waited in the shadows to fulfill your dread.

Until the time you take your true place

To destroy those who banish us where we hid our face.

Through this ritual we hide you in this precious stone

To last beyond the years and curse the one whom it owns.

When one day you come back to call

We will avenge those who brought your fall."

The woman standing over the stone altar collapsed as she dropped the parchment scroll onto the ground and the other woman in the semi circle fell backward as the fire in the room suddenly went out. A bright red glow in the middle of the stone lit up the room and Isabelle saw the same red ruby from the chalice burning a bright light

118

through the room. She looked closer and saw the resemblance to the sea glass stones she found from the beach. As she stepped forward, the light from the stone went out and the room fell dark. She stood silent when she felt hands grasp each of her shoulders. The fingernails dug into her skin, and she let out a cry of pain.

A small fire lit around the stone, and she felt the rancid breath of the old woman holding the parchment on her face. "You have been chosen, my dear. The piedra rojo has travelled many places through time but it has finally chosen you."

Isabelle jumped back in pain and fell to the ground as she escaped the grasp of the old woman. Again, she awoke in a sweat although this time, it was on the uncomfortable desk in her workshop. She pulled back the sleeve on her shirt exposing three small claw marks across her shoulder. Slowly, she let the shirt snap back into place as she stared down at the beautiful necklace that lay on the table almost complete. It sparkled and seemed to glow as she felt her gaze fall on it. The dreams raced back into her head, and she knew she needed to get rid of that necklace, and those pieces of ruby stone but she just could not force her hand to reach down and dispose of it.

Instead, she reached over and picked up the last part of the gold chain and began putting the necklace together. So absorbed into her project, Isabelle failed to acknowledge the alarm sounding in the bedroom alerting her of her impending time to get ready for work. She also lost track of time during the day as she ignored the several phone calls from work checking in on her. The longer she worked on the necklace the more transfixed she became and the more she knew she could never part with it.

As the clock reached almost seven at night, she was startled by a knock at the door. She looked up surprised to discover that the morning sun she first noticed was now replaced by a half moon and darkness outside. *Have I been here all day?* Rising from the chair to answer the annoying knock on her door. Isabelle opened the door to find her friend, Brooke, from work standing with a concerned look on her face.

"Where have you been? I have been worried about you all day. You can't answer your phone?" She blasted Isabelle as she entered the house throwing off her jacket.

Isabelle stuttered as she backed toward her work desk to hide the necklace, "I, I, I was just busy, that's all." She faced Brooke trying to block the necklace from her view, a jealous anxiety suddenly overtaking her.

Brooke walked towards her confused and tried to peek around her to see what she was hiding. "What is it, Isabelle? What is that behind you?" Brooke jerked quickly around catching a glimpse of the ruby sea glass as it began to glow.

"Wow, what is that? It is beautiful." Brooke said almost in a trance as she reached for the necklace.

Isabelle swiped at her arm scratching the side of her wrist as Brooke let out a cry jumping back. Isabelle screamed with fire in her eyes, "It is mine! La mujer de rojo! The Woman of Red is mine! My life for her."

Isabelle placed the necklace around her neck and the red sea glass burned a bright crimson transforming her once youthful smile into an ancient wizened old sneer with a wrinkled and pale face. She rose up above Brooke towering over her as she looked down speaking in anger over the frightened woman.

"It is time, my friends. I call on you now to avenge me from the ones who caused my fall. The stone has finally found its home."

120

Brooke looked to her right and saw a small light from a fire burning from Isabelle's living room and heard the rustle of footsteps approaching. She looked in horror as several frail old women in dark crimson cloaks entered the room stationing themselves around Isabelle. The group was chanting in a soft hum in old Latin phrases, their eyes glowing as red as the cloaks they wore. Isabelle raised her hands above her head and the group went silent. As she stood Brooke noticed the necklace that once contained six separate pieces of red sea glass had now transformed into a single large ruby stone that hung from the middle of the necklace.

Isabelle shouted out in an incomprehensible tone before lowering her head and her arms and looking directly at Brooke. "The stone calls for a sacrifice my friends, and before us sits a willing volunteer. Brought of her own free will, she will be the first to answer for our vengeance."

Isabelle closed her eyes, and the stone glowed a bright red as the lights in the house went dark. Brooke screamed in horror as the glow of the stone encompassed around her as it fed on her. The women covered in the crimson cloaks surrounded her as she lay on the floor and a bright light illuminated the entire room, as Brooke was absorbed into the stone forever.

All around Isabelle, the woman began chanting, "Woman of Red, Mujer de Roja," over and over. "I have become that which was destroyed so long ago. I am once again the Woman of Red."

The Woman of Red raised her arms. "It is time for our vengeance. Those who wronged us in the past will now be held accountable."

As she spoke the Red Stone pulsed, a portal appeared in the kitchen. On the other side of the gateway a forest became visible, dark with the exception of several fires burning up long stakes. The Woman of Red looked out with sadness as she fixated on one of the stakes on fire. It contained a woman screaming out in pain. The face staring back at her sensed recognition and then despite her pain formed a smile on her face. The Woman of Red led the group out through the portal onto the field of burning stakes as now several more women appeared burning as the fires were lit.

In the background, villagers screamed as they saw the group of women appear out of nowhere. "Witches," one cried out as they ran in fear. The Woman of Red approached the woman burning in the middle of the formation raising her hands to stop the fire as the Red Stone burned bright.

"Come down my sisters, for this is our vengeance." She cried out as she stared at the woman looking down at her. They both smiled as she stared back up at an identical face.

"The Red Stone has taken me back to avenge my own death."

The group of women clad in the crimson cloaks gathered around the woman on the stake in amazement as they stared at not one but two of the Woman of Red.

Stephen Johnson

Stephen Johnson is a retired Naval Officer, husband, father, and Chihuahua dad serving 22 years on four different ships over his career. Jumpmaster Press will publish his first novel, The Fizz Prophecy, in 2022. His short stories appear in anthologies from Scare Street's Night Terrors Volume 8 and 17, No Bad Books' Released, and Breaking Rules Europe's Death Ship.

Lose the Battle, Win the War
By: Donna J. W. Munro

A DOCTOR, A priest, and a judge walk into the bar.

Rosie watched them make their way through the Saturday night crowd. She turned to pour the three ales they'd want and to dip up three bowls of mutton stew. She whispered to the other bar wench and her sister witch, Sarah, that she'd serve the three.

She made her way through the drunken propositions and the pinches on her ass toward the table of powerful men she'd been tasked to observe.

"Your lordships," she said, putting the tankards and the brimming bowls before them.

They never laid their hands on her or said anything disrespectful. They weren't like the common men with a bit of coin and too much ale in their stomach. That was one kind of dangerous.

These were the other kind.

"Thanks, Rosie. Water the ale if you would. We have

great things to talk about tonight. After the meal, we'll retire to the back," Bishop Orto said, eyes smiling with the crow footed humor of his age.

She nodded and headed back to air out their room.

Unlike the rooms upstairs that they let out to travelers by the night for some, by the hour for others, the room for the three men she served was rented indefinitely for a huge sum. She unlocked the heavy door they'd had installed and opened the window that was encased in iron bars.

Iron to keep out the magics.

Fools.

The table had been dusted that morning and the room smelled honestly of the things inside. Leather bound scrolls, sheets of velum, sharpened reeds of pine, and the sweet smell of iron gall ink they'd ordered from the apothecary.

And underneath it all, hints of the herbs she and her sister had hidden around the room.

Bindings.

Curses.

Anything to keep the men's work from becoming…

The door snicked open as she stoked up the fire in the small hearth.

The doctor, James Porter of London, entered and pulled the large Bible from the shelf.

Bishop Orto took his place at the table, stirring the ink with a reed and whispering the prayer he said every time they worked.

Only Judge Matthewson nodded to her. He saw everything and noted her every move.

It made him the most dangerous among them.

126

"Another round, m'lords?" She asked, curtsying as was expected.

"Thank you, Rosie," he said, turning to the work before them.

Rosie pulled the door shut and headed to the room next-door. One of the other witches lay on a pallet next to the wall, deep in meditation. Normally the Orto's prayer would keep her from spirit walking into the room, but the curses and charms they'd hidden gave her the ability to listen closely to the doings of the three.

The Goddesses told them that theirs was vile work.

But Rosie was afraid there was nothing to be done.

She put her hand against the wall and felt the pulse of power shifting.

She collected the watered ale and made her way back into the room.

"Here it is. Suffer not a...m'khashepah–"

The judge and the doctor leaned in and studied the Hebrew word and compared it to the Greek and then the Latin.

"It's damning alright," the judge said.

Rosie put the ale at his elbow hoping he'd knock into it and wash the words they copied away.

The Goddesses had told them that these three were the breaking point.

Nothing would be the same.

"Could be poisoner," the Bishop said. "Or Witch could be a worker of miracles without the word of God. Paul spoke of magic without God in..."

Rosie left before the priest could quote even one more

word from the damned book.

She made her way out of the inn, throwing her apron down and running to the woods. To the sacred glen. She stripped to sky clad and called the corners so that she'd be hidden with the Goddess.

"It is as you said. They have come to kill us all!"

The Goddess appeared as a kneeling girl petting the clover, so flowers sprouted in a thick carpet around her.

"You must understand so that you can protect the sisters," the Goddess said.

"I understand the church... we're an affront to their commandments, but we've stayed out of their way, in the woods and—"

"Soon they will cut down the woods."

Rosie nodded. The woods were wild and full of old sprites. Endangered folk and creatures who'd lose the doors from their world to ours if the church had a say.

"But doctors? We've shared our herbs and taught them what we know. They've pushed us aside until we are just doctoring women. Why do they care?"

The Goddess transformed into a heavy mother near her quickening and so green with life. "Daughter, half the world is being doctored by witches. That's competition!"

Rosie thought about the male doctors and their backward beliefs about women. How terrible it would be to let them deliver the babies or care for the women's complaints. Tears ran down her cheeks as she realized the inevitability of their being pushed aside.

"And the judge? We don't meddle in their doings."

The Goddess grayed and stood as crone with her withered fingers clutched into arthritic fists. "Think girl.

What do they gain?"

Rosie closed her eyes and thought on it.

She called the truth out of the mist and saw it full of gallows, stones, racks, and fires... and judges.

Judges would be the instrument of their elimination.

"We have to stop them!" Rosie said.

The Triple Goddess stood before her joined and resplendent... all women and none. Beyond and her and everywhere at once.

"They will not win the war, Rosie. You must believe that even in the ash and the darkness," she said, then enfolded rose in a six-armed embrace. "Do as you must to these men, but what they believe... it can't be killed. It is a pestilence that will run its course."

Then Rosie was alone.

"It will run its course, but not in my time," Rosie said, understanding what the Goddess meant.

She dressed and hurried back to the inn. She passed her sisters, the cooks and maids and wenches working. She went to the watered ale and dropped sweet toad venom in the cups.

She brought the ale into the men, who in her absence had set to outlining their war against witches.

Orto drank the ale with relish, wetting his mouth as Doctor Porter scribbled his last words down.

"A toast, brothers," Porter said as he lay down the quill. "To a faithful, profitable future for all men."

The bishop took another hearty drink and smiled. "Hear, hear. Important work. The final conversion of our lands. A true Christendom for the work to come."

Judge Matthewson nodded and sipped, watching Rosie in the corner.

Her cheeks were red, but she kept her smile pleasant.

The bishop would go down soon from all he'd drunk.

Then Porter would follow.

But Matthewson?

The judge announced he had to piss.

Rosie wished he'd had more of the drink.

Maybe he'd fall into the privy hole so she wouldn't have to do more harm.

She followed, watching as he wove slowly through the crowd and out into the courtyard.

She found pissing against the fence like a common man.

He didn't turn to face her when he said, "Followed me out, Rosie?"

Tucking his part back in with a respect usually not paid bar wenches, he turned to face her.

"Sorry sir, I thought you might need–"

"I know your game, little witch. I smelled the difference between the first ale and the third. Me thinks the bishop and the good doctor are breathing their last. I didn't but sip it, so maybe I'll live. Maybe I won't. But our work will."

She heard the front door of the inn slam and the thundering hooves of a fast horse from beyond the courtyard fence.

"That's my rider. I gave him the plans we made tonight."

He smiled and wobbled as the toad poison made its way to his heart muscle, seizing it in an iron grip.

"I may die, Rosie, but our ideas won't."

130

Blood bubbled at his lips as he laughed. He stumbled to one knee and fell on his side.

Rose ran over and gathered him into her lap, to watch the light leave his eyes.

From inside her, the Goddess bloomed like a triple-headed iris, full of green, blue, and vivid yellow. Too many eyes to focus on but three sets of lips speaking the same words.

"Your idea has a short life, Judge. Your kind will take some of my daughters, but mostly you'll make yourselves into villains harassing innocents. I see futures farther than you can know. My daughters will survive and your kind… You will be an embarrassment."

Then she closed his eyes and let the toad poison do its slow, painful work.

She parted from Rosie's body and stood beside her.

"The Hammer of Witches comes. It is only delayed by this act," the Goddess said.

Rosie nodded and knelt, ready to take her punishment for causing harm.

"There is a balance, daughter. Your act ended life but gave you time to save your sisters. Send them this message. The judges are coming. We must hide. Keep the secret traditions but hide in plain sight. We will survive. In this, you balance your debt." Then the flowering triple head smiled at Rosie, a sight of such terrible beauty she gasped.

The judges would win many battles.

But Rosie knew they'd lose the war.

That was enough.

She dusted off her knees and went about closing the inn, driving out all the drunkards into the streets.

She and her sisters had much work to do.

Donna J. W. Munro

Donna J. W. Munro's pieces are published in Nothing's Sacred Magazine IV and V, Corvid Queen, *Hazard Yet Forward* (2012), *Enter the Apocalypse* (2017), *Beautiful Lies, Painful Truths II* (2018), *Terror Politico* (2019), *It Calls from the Forest* (2020), *Gray Sisters Vol 1*(2020), *Borderlands Vol 7* (2020), *Pseudopod 752* (2021), and others. Check out her first novel, *Revelation: Poppet Cycle Book 1*. Contact her at https://www.donnajwmunro.com or @DonnaJWMunro on Twitter.

The Banshee Tavern
By: Melissa Small

THIS IS A story about a living old Stone Tavern named 'The Banshee' and I do mean living. The Banshee is alive just like you. Have you ever stepped inside a building and felt like you were being watched? Chances are you have been in a magical building, and you were being watched by the building. Buildings like The Banshee have gender pronouns just like us; in this case The Banshee is a she / her building. No one knows how or why this happens or how they express their preference, it just happens.

The Banshee is one of these buildings; she is the youngest of all the magical buildings being built in 1927 by a Witch to shelter her coven and other magical beings from the mortals. I think I should mention that Witch is now a gender-neutral term. It applies equally to male and female practitioners of the mystical arts. Most mortals have a dislike for anything that does not fit in their reality. That means magic, the unusual or unexplainable. There are a few other buildings around the world like The Banshee built for similar reasons but this story, as I have said earlier is about

The Banshee.

The Banshee is not the easiest place to find. If you are not looking for her you will not find her. In this tale she is located in the Toronto underground PATH. Upon entering The Banshee there is a sign. This is the only common thing the magical buildings have.

The Banshee is protected and governed under the Weapons Pact of 1945.

Witch and Magical Being Sanctuary

No Warlocks

No Weapons – Mortal or Otherwise

No Fighting – Magical or Otherwise

No Curses.

Violation of any or all of these rules is punishable by death.

You might have noticed that mortals are not banned from The Banshee. Indeed, many patrons of these magical buildings are mortals. Well just the ones who are more open minded than most. A secondary sign is also visible from the door.

No Shoes

No Shirt.

No Magical Hats

No Service.

No one is quite sure where this sign came from, but it appeared one night after a particularly rowdy patron pulled more than just rabbits out of their hat. Personally, I think The Banshee put it there herself.

The Banshee is like most other old-world taverns you have seen. Dim lighting with an oval bar surrounded by stools with a few tables scattered throughout the remaining floor space. Mounted around the walls are various paintings and animal trophies. By far the most impressive and slightly disturbing is the Ethereal stag's head. If you watch it closely you can see it shimmering in and out of our reality. It is best if you do not look at it too long and it is liable to give you a headache and well, it doesn't like to be stared at.

Hanging from the ceiling there are some unique chandeliers. No two are the same though the designs are similar. They have that gothic look to them but are made from bone. They could be human, witch, some other magical being or possibly even demon bones. And the light comes from a luminescent glow emanating from the bones themselves.

Behind the bar lists the available drinks. There are all the usual mortal drinks available but for those who can see them there are various types of brews and potions also available. That's where you will find me. Master Brew Witch Skye Devonshire at your service. I attend to Banshee's guests and make sure everyone has a good time and obeys the rules.

In total there are four bartenders or Brew Witches. Each one of us are masters in a particular type of elemental brewing. I'm the Fire Brewer. If you like your drinks on the hot and fiery side, you come see me. I can make you an Aurora Sunshine that could melt your heart.... well, if you were human that would happen. Magical folks like their drinks with a bit spicier side.

The Banshee is divided into two areas. The first is the bar establishment that I have already described. The second is the Den. The Den is accessed through a stone archway at the back of The Banshee. Two Wardens, magical stone constructs that keep unwanted beings from entering The Den. Mortals are strictly prohibited. Most mortals see the Wardens as really buff guys, like the wrestlers on TV.

The Den is an interesting place managed by The Banshee herself. It is a space that can form into whatever is required, large open spaces, small individual rooms, concert hall, banquet area and more. It can be several or all of these things at once. The Witch never designed this space; it just appeared one day in 1972. It didn't just appear in The Banshee but in every living building throughout the mortal and magical realms. The archway can also be used for travel between the buildings if you know how and both buildings are willing.

This tale is about a night not too long ago where The Den, all its magical brethren and very possibly the entire world was almost lost forever. It was a particularly slow night. Only one of the Brew Witches was required to work that night. Don't know if it was luck or divine intervention but it happened to be me.

It was almost closing time, and I was brewing a Volcanic Daiquiri for a customer when I saw a mortal heading for the archway. Didn't think much about it, as the Wardens would turn him away. I passed the drink to the customer and put the coins in the till when I noticed. No Wardens, where were they? I should have reacted faster, but the Wardens were always there.

Then it really happened, a mortal walked through the archway. Then all hell broke loose. I leaped from my position behind the bar and rushed the archway. The archway flashed and the charred corpse of the mortal shot back into The Banshee. Not sure if The Banshee or the Witches in the Den were responsible.

Patrons gathered around the mortal remains shocked at what had happened. People were tossing theories left and right as to who or what killed him and where had the Wardens gone.

The doors suddenly blew off their hinges. I swear I heard The Banshee scream in pain. Three Warlocks stepped into The Banshee. Warlocks are Witches that have sold their souls to Demons for power. Demons are explainer entities that use mortals and Witches to enter our world. This deal with Demons makes Warlocks unwelcome in the civilized magical world. They generally dress in hooded robes, as these three were, to hide their disfigurements from dealing with Demons.

So, there they were three Warlocks standing inside The Banshee. I spoke the panic spell. The lights brighten to full intensity, all the doors and windows (except the front door) are magically sealed, the magical authorities notified, and all of the patrons are teleported outside.

I held out my hand and a simple magical staff appeared there. This I know is from The Banshee and she has done this for me in the past. That's another story for later. I ran for the Archway to get between them and the Den. There was no way I was letting a bunch of mangy Warlocks enter.

I was too slow again, one second the Warlocks were at the door next they were at the archway stepping through. Again, I thought I heard The Banshee groan in pain. I darted forward and through the archway into the Den. I was greeted by a horrific site, bodies everywhere so many of my magical brethren torn to pieces, like paper going through a shredder.

The room I stood in was a vast empty space. I couldn't

see any walls or the ceiling. For a second, I saw the Warlocks heading towards a crowd of witches then a concealing mist swept into the space. It wasn't the first time I wished that I could communicate with The Banshee. Was the fog made by The Banshee to conceal me from the Warlocks? Or did the Warlocks make it to conceal themselves from me?

Heedlessly I ran forward in the direction of the figures emerging from the fog startling both Witches and Warlocks alike. So, the fog was from The Banshee after all. There was the High Sacerdos of all Witches flanked by the four Elemental Masters. Not like me. I am only a Brew Witch these guys are the masters of the elements themselves. Facing them was the Warlocks.

I swung my staff like a baseball bat at the nearest of the three uttering "Impetu." The Warlock flew back and collided with a wall that was not there a second ago. Tendrils emerged from the wall and surrounded the Warlock. The wall then descended back into the floor taking its prisoner with it. Score one for The Banshee. The remaining two Warlocks screamed in fury and turned towards me.

The other two Warlocks hissed and looked at me. The one on the right tossed a nasty looking seed pod in my direction. Vines burst out from the pod in midair and came hurtling in my direction. I pointed my staff at it and said with as much force as I could 'Ortus." Light burst out from the tip of my staff incinerating the vine monster and continued on to the Warlock who threw it. The Warlock brought his hands up to protect himself from the light. He took a step back and fell into a hole that was not there before. Score two for The Banshee.

And here I bet you thought a building couldn't fight. Well, let me tell you The Banshee can, and she doesn't take too kindly to beings invading her personal space. The remaining Warlock gaped at where his compatriot used to be and said "Irappu." His body collapsed into a ball of light and shot forward past the Elemental Masters and engulfed the High Sacerdos. She screamed in agony and then crumpled into a pile of ash and cinder. Our most high one was gone.

I stood there in shock with the Masters. I could feel the Banshee sorrow as well. Exhaustion overtook me. I am not a spell slinger you know. I make drinks for a living, not used to the high intensity magic. I dropped to my knees and began to cry. I looked up to see the four Master's standing over me.

"Where were the Wardens?" One of them asked me. I barely heard him. It felt like a nightmare, and I just wanted to wake up.

"I don't know," I replied softly. "I was making a brew and I looked over and saw a mortal, it wasn't until a second or two later I noticed the Wardens weren't at their post."

"We must alert the other Sanctuaries." They said and left me there on my knees in shame. Four magical doorways appeared and each of them stepped through a different door.

Somehow, I returned to my spot behind the bar. It was empty of everyone. Though hot cocoa was on the counter, my favorite mortal drink. "Thank you" I whispered to The Banshee and scooped it up into my hands.

How did this happen? Where were the Wardens? What was happening in the Den tonight? It was then that Dylan Wolfe, chief of the local authorities came barging in with a squad of his goons. Dylan is actually a pretty good guy for a Dark Elf.

He came over to the bar and there was a second cup of

cocoa there waiting. He pulled up a stool and eyed the drink suspiciously. "Already talked to everyone outside. Tell me what happened in the Den." So, I told him the story I just told you word for word.

"Where are the dead Warlocks?" and The Banshee made a groaning noise, and two mangled corpses were spit up out of the floor at Dylan's feet.

"I suspect that is what is left of them sir."

Dylan waved his team over and they took the bodies away. "So how did a Brew Witch do that to Warlocks?"

"I had help from The Banshee" I replied.

"You are a Brew Witch not a Warden." He said and pushed himself back away from the bar. "Why get involved? You should have left it to the experts."

"The experts were either dead or exhausted. Besides, it was my shift, so it was my responsibility."

Dylan pushed back from the bar and walked to the archway. Oddly, he couldn't pass through. "I need access to the Den, can you please let me pass?" he asked The Banshee.

The Banshee then did something I had never seen before. The archway covered in a mist and then began to replay the event inside like a mortal movie. Dylan stood still viewing the events that unfolded in the Den including my own contributions

"I see you don't follow protocol. "Dylan noted.

"As I said this happened on my watch." I told him. "My shift, my responsibility. "

"Humph. This is demon magic you shouldn't be..." Dylan stopped speaking when he saw me cast Ortus. "That's a Warden spell. You shouldn't even be able to cast that." Dylan stared at me for a full minute without speaking. "Ah, I see the family resemblance now. Warden Tarn Devonshire was your father. Your father was an icon. We grieved at his loss all those years ago."

The tableau unfolding in the archway continued. I turned away when the Warlock turned into a ball of light. "The one that attacked the Sacerdos was a Shadow Demon. The poor fool's soul who allowed it into our world would be vaporized when it left the body to attack the Sacerdos."

The mist in the archway faded "These are not low-end Warlocks. They were all trained assassins. You are lucky to be alive, Brew Witch."

"Luck had nothing to do with it. I had the help of The Banshee and the skill my dad taught me." It was at that moment I realized Dylan was right, I could have been killed.

"This is not over yet. We will find the Shadow Demon and put an end to its plans. But with your contribution we have at least put a crimp in their plans. The Elemental Masters are still alive and raising the alarm throughout the magical community." Dylan turned and headed out.

"Let me help you." I spoke before I had time to think about it.

"But you are helping. This is your place to protect." Dylan waved his arms around "The Banshee needs you." The Banshee whistled in agreement as Dylan walked out the door.

Then I saw The Banshee with a different perspective. She is my friend, and my friend needs my help. Her friends need my help. My friend and my responsibility. I Master Brew Witch Skye Devonshire swear to protect this place and its patrons. And Warlocks beware, you are not welcome in my world.

Melissa Small

Melissa Small is a mother of two boys and her husband also shares all her nerdy hobbies. She has published seven short stories. A story in the book, The Way Through by Polar Expressions Publishing (Fate of the Sea Witch), Futuristic Canada by Dark Helix Press (Poutine, Bugs and Big Bessie) and five short stories in The World of Myth Magazine, (Wool of Time, Boom, Soleless and two SeaWitch stories).

Island Time
By: Victory Witherkeigh

THE FLUTTERING OF tiny wings and a constant buzzing zone in and out of my ears morning after morning just as I wake up.

I've never owned an alarm clock. This sound has always greeted me each morning. I look out to see the gathering black moths flying just outside my bedroom window. They flit and flutter back and forth as if the cacophony of their wings announces their presence. And they should, for my people know these bugs as the fluttering souls of the dead moving on.

I was only a small child when they first came to me, drawing a hush from my parents and Mama Tita as they landed on my skin. I giggled in the prickly warm, lush grass, their antenna tickling my fingers and toes as we sunbathed together.

"Psst!" My mother said with a hiss. "Do not move... those are the black witch moths!"

I remember seeing my mother's face, pale with her

mouth gaped open like a fish about to be eaten alive.

"But they're so friendly…" I giggled back.

"They are the signs of Death!" My mother said, her lips thinning. "They are not a toy!"

"Hush!" Mama Tita shushed her, "It is a gift…"

Staring down at creatures crawling on my body, they were a lot larger than any other butterfly I had ever seen. Some moths flapped their wings down, almost covering my entire forearm. Their wingspan was large enough to share the shape of a bat or a small bird, with the black mosaic patterns showcasing hints of blue and brown in some tinting.

Just as quickly as they said hello, they fluttered off into the sky again. The adults sprinted towards me, dragging me to the local healers and priests to drive the "bad omens" away.

As I grew older, I simply learned to stop mentioning the morning moths or -how the beating of their wings and little hearts would keep me up at night, or waking me from my dreams. Mama Tita told me our dreams are where our souls can leave the body and float into the other realms of the spirit, be it good or ill. When I was awake, my heart never seemed to adjust back to actual life.

"You're always running on island time," Mama Tita would say, "Always ten, fifteen, twenty minutes late like your mother…"

"Mom says that it's called 'fashionably late.'" I'd sass back, annoyed that no matter what I tried to do to get a good night's sleep or how hard I tried to ignore the moths, it never seemed to help me get out of the door on time.

I know they didn't believe me when I told them I have trouble sleeping, that the reason I'm late is always that I'm constantly grasping every second of sleep. I can get that waking myself up is nearly impossible.

"It's like trying to wake the dead..." My family would mutter after shaking me and yelling my name to get me to move.

If they only knew how valid those words were...

Every night, from the time I was a child, I'd dreamt of people. I don't dream about adventures or fantasy worlds with these people. No, I dreamt, night after night, about their deaths. No matter what I've tried over the years - teas, herbs, drugs, the dreams come. Some nights, it's just flickers of their faces just before it happens. Other times, I'm a fly on the wall as their bodies lay on the cold, steel slab of the hospital morgues. I'd stare down as the hard, sterile metal first carves into their chilled skin, carving their chests like a frozen chicken breast with the steel grating against the icicles between the fat and muscle tissue.

Mama Tita, my nanny, housekeeper, and essential second mother, watched day after day, year after year, as the night sweats and tears soaked my bedspreads to the mattress liners. She wiped the tears from my face as I tossed and turned, kicking, screaming, and begging to be allowed to sleep in her bed instead of by myself.

"Shhhh," she'd whisper, "I know it's scary, having this gift..."

Even then, she saw nothing to do with me as evil, despite what our people said about what bad luck it was to see the dead in your dreams.

"I have to believe that there's a purpose to it. A reason that you have this gift - a chance to do good. Just as I have been blessed to have you, I have my surrogate baby, my child, even though I've never married or been pregnant. They have blessed me with the good fortune to help

147

others... maybe that's you're calling also..." Mama would say, stroking my hair as I cried into her camisole lace tops, day after day.

Not that she wasn't tough as nails or allowed me to be spoiled. Oh no, Mama Tita knew that the coddling could only go so far before she'd remind me to put my big girl panties on and handle myself.

Over the years, it's meant that any time I can sleep without those images allows for the weight on my shoulders to drop, the pressure to keep those secrets and anxiety to myself melting off my shoulders as though stepping out of a pool with the water cascading off my back. These treasured moments of silence, peace, and tranquility carried my mind through the endless hours of twilight blinks and sunrises with no reprieve from the sounds of buzzing. On those mornings and events, I was late, Mama Tita would always smooth things over for me.

"She's young," she'd tell the people annoyed with my tardiness, most often my parents or teachers, "She's running an errand for me, but she'll be here..."

"Don't worry, I would know if something was wrong - I can always feel if she's okay. If anything happened to her, I would feel it in my bones," she'd say before I came barreling through the door with whatever excuses and gripes I had for the day.

It's only now that I'm stuck in traffic that my perpetual lateness seems to be the worst payback for my delinquencies as a kid.

For all these years that I've grown and honed my magic to control the visions, to use it for good, it never made a difference when the pandemic hit. I thought I had endured the worst moments of my life with the passing of my grandmothers. They completely surprised me when I was

148

called about their demise. In all the visions I'd ever had, I had never seen their faces in the dreams. I thought my heart would have shattered through my chest when the nurse contacted me, my blood pounding in my ears that one had passed from a stroke. I only have memories of collapsing against the drywall of my office, sobbing on the floor.

What kind of cruel joke was this? To see the deaths of the masses coming, but not my flesh and blood?

Then, just a year later, my Lola passed in her sleep. Once again, no warning, no vision, no signal. Just waking up to the phone ringing, the gasping shock, and tears as I tried to pull her socks onto her feet as the tears clouded my vision.

I cried in Mama Tita's arms, wailing that I was a failure, a joke of a lifetime in my inability to help them, soothe them, or be there with them in the last moments.

"No, no," she shushed me, patting my dark brown hair as I cried my salty tears into her sleeves once more, "They loved you with everything they had. They would be so proud of you - just like I am..."

It took so many years of therapy to process those words of Mama Tita. I thought I had overcome the worst, processed my guilt and shame with my latest set of shaman instructors and Wiccan guides to help me hone on these dreams. Nothing can prepare the strongest of us who practice our craft in the realms of dreams and the lands of the dead for a mass onslaught of death.

When the virus began spreading, my dreams became flooded with the crackling noise of plastic unwrapping. White-hot flashes of light blinked in and out of my vision as my chest constricted. Everything felt hot, achy, my bones and joints as though the cartilage was disintegrating with every breath I gasped for. In the distance were faint echoes of voices yelling, "Code Blue," mixed with the incessant beeping. Each morning, my eardrums would echo as I shook my clammy, sweaty head to clear my mind. The noises would grow and compound night after night, the people's faces angry, screaming vitriol as they passed on about hoaxes and fear. As the news coverage spread, we begged Mama Tita to stay home, each of us taking turns to bring her groceries, medicine, and even new books and magazines to read. I knew she was lonely, that she was so used to being out and about in the world, but we all thought we could keep her as safe as possible.

It still didn't make it any easier when her face appeared in my dreams just after Thanksgiving.

No, no, no... I thought to myself as I dialed her at three in the morning.

There was no answer on the phone. I called her neighbor, a friend of hers in the same apartment complex, to see if she could get ahold of her.

"Oi!" her neighbor groggily answered, "I was just about to call you! Mama Tita isn't feeling well... I've called an ambulance..."

I didn't even wait for the woman to finish before I called my mother, demanding to know what was happening. Apparently, Mama had been feeling ill for a few days but only called her that evening to say they scared her it was COVID.

By the morning light creeping into my bedroom as my footprints melded into my plush area rug, the doctors were alerting us that her test came back positive, and they needed to transfer her to ICU.

Everything around me seemed to spin, both in slow motion and at the speed of light. I refused to sleep the first few nights, terrified of seeing her face again. The mornings became more agitating as the calls from the hospital remained the same.

"She's intubated, no change. We are doing everything we can. You may drop off any framed photos you'd like her to have, and we can put them up along her isolation area for her to see..."

Going through her photos only allowed the stabbing pains in my chest to get more profound as the hours dragged. My family kept saying to pray but brace myself for the inevitable.

"Mama Tita at least had her will and power of attorney in place," my mother said as I stared vacantly at the wall, "She made everything so easy - she's got her entire funeral planned out. She'd even picked a casket last year..."

"Yeah, but that doesn't mean that she was ready to go!" I hissed back, "She was just prepared, like she always is, making sure that we're taken care of... that she's never a problem..."

The cycle seemed endless, a rollercoaster ride of hope and despair. A week into the hospital stay, she improved. Her vital signs were steady enough as they transferred her to a lower unit. I could only stare into a Zoom screen, trying to impart my will that she tried to fight.

"I will, my love," she said, breathing heavily with each word, "But I want you to still let me be the one to care for you..."

I had thought that my gift, this omen, was finally going to be of use. I told her it was a gift. She said my gift had told me to call her that night. It's all I can think of now, as my knees fidget and tremble at the stoplight in this dark January night.

The hospital called and told me Mama Tita took a turn - that it looked like she wouldn't make it after all. I grip the steering wheel, trying to will my feet to stay on the brake pedal instead of the gas.

I can't be late... I can't be late... Please... Please...

The green light just flickers, and I hit the gas, flooring it down the road. It's as if I blink, and I'm racing on the pavement, standing outside a hospital window, staring at the woman who shaped my world, my heart, and my life.

Mama... look...

I can't even speak. I'm crying so hard... barely thinking as I see the heartbeat monitor stop—the nurses and doctors standing by with her orders for no extraordinary measures.

My fingers tap the glass, trying to make some sound forward from my vocal cords. It's only then that I see it. A black witch moth was now nestled in the outer pane of the window, staring at me as I started to fall apart.

Mama Tita... look... for once... I'm on time...

Victory Witherkeigh

Victory Witherkeigh is a female Filipino author originally from Los Angeles, CA, and currently living in the Las Vegas area. Victory was a finalist for Killer Nashville's 2020 Claymore Award, an Honoree for Cinnamon Press's 2020 Literature Award, and Wingless Dreamer's 2020 Overcoming Fear Short Story award. She has print publications in the horror anthologies *Supernatural Drabbles of Dread* through Macabre Ladies Publishing, *Bodies Full of Burning* through Sliced Up Press, and *In Filth It Shall Be Found* through OutCast Press. She also has a literary short story in *Overcoming Fear* through Wingless Dreamers.

More From Zombie Works Publications!

MONSTERTHOLOGY
VOL. 1

YOU CAN'T KILL ME, I'M
ALREADY DEAD

A DARK WORLD OF THE
SPIRITS AND THE FEY

ZOMBIE EPICDEMIC

MONSTERTHOLOGY
VOL. 2

FULL MOON & HOWLIN:
A WEREWOLF ANTHOLOGY

WWW.MYTHMART.COM

www.ingramcontent.com/pod-product-compliance
Lightning Source LLC
Chambersburg PA
CBHW071939170626
46813CB00005B/1787